THE WRONG DECISION

DANYELLE SCROGGINS

PUBLISHING
WWW.DANYELLESCROGGINS.COM
Email: jdstovelovepownpublishing@gmail.com

"Scripture quotations taken from the New American Standard Bible®, Copyright © 1960, 1962, 1963, 1968, 1971, 1972, 1973, 1975, 1977, 1995 by The Lockman Foundation

Used by permission." (www.Lockman.org)

Published by: Divinely Sown Publishing

THE WRONG DECISION

A *LOUISIANA LOVE BOOK 2*

Copyright © 2020 by Danyelle Scroggins

A LOUISIANA LOVE BOOK 2

First Edition paperback

10 9 8 7 6 5 4 3 2 1

Printed in the United States of America

Book Cover Design by Danyelle Scroggins

Cover Model: Lexus Antwine

Exclusive discounts are available for quantity purchases. For details, contact the publisher at the address above.

Printed in the United States of America

✿ Created with Vellum

Dedicated to

To Ms. Josephine Brown, you have been more than a friend, and I'm so grateful to have you in my corner. Thanks for keeping me centered...especially when I stray to far to the left. Accountability is the fruit of friendship and I love you for making me always accountable to the Word I preach.
Danyelle

ALSO BY DANYELLE SCROGGINS

WHERE THE BOOTH/JACKSON & KIMBREL FAMILY BEGAN

A Louisiana Christmas:

Love Me Again (Book 1)

Never Looking Back (Book 2)

Same Families Continued Stories...

A Louisiana Love Series

The Right Choice

*The Wrong Decision

The Perfect Chance (Coming Soon)

"But the wisdom that is from above is first pure, then peaceable, gentle, easy to be intreated, full of mercy and good fruits, without partiality, and without hypocrisy."

James 3:17

CHAPTER 1

Veronica laid her head on Kane's sofa's arm and stretched her left foot across his legs. All the stress of the past few months was beginning to take a toll on her. So much had changed since December.

Her mother and brother were both married, her cousin Selena was now living with her, and she was spending much more time at Kane's house.

"Give me your other foot," Kane said, giving her left foot a little nudge, reaching for and securing her right foot as she complied.

The Regina Rochelle body scrub was a little gift from heaven, and along with Kane's hands, the product was working magic.

The good thing was it felt so good, but the bad thing—her body was reacting in ways she would've never expected. Had it not been for Vance and his little incident, she would have been married in February and doing precisely what married people were blessed to do.

But now, here she was in mid-May, longing. Filled with passions beyond her explanation and praying for an escape.

Kane's hands were now moving up her leg, massaging her ankles, then her calf, and now her inner thigh.

Oh God, if you don't provide an escape for me, I'm going to forfeit all those promises I made to You.

Ring. Ring.

"Would you pass me my phone?" Veronica asked as Kane was already reaching for her phone lying on the coffee table in front of them.

"Hello," Veronica answered. "Okay, give me a minute or two, and I'll be right there." She pressed the red button to disconnect the call.

"Babe, Selena needs me. Thank you for the foot rub."

"You're welcome. But are you sure you need to go?"

"Yes, Kane, because if I don't leave now, I'm going to have a burnt place."

She wanted to say, "The Lord has given me an escape and this escapee is running," but she didn't.

"Okay, baby, he leaned into her kiss."

"I love you, and I'll see you tomorrow."

"Okay, Vee, goodnight."

Veronica quickly walked out of the door without even looking into Kane's eyes or before anything else could happen. A deep longing and lustful passions were beginning to get the best of her; no, them. Kane wasn't the only one guilty.

She opened the door and went straight into the kitchen.

Before she could even address Selena, she laid her back against the refrigerator and began to say, "Thank You, Jesus. Thank You, Jesus."

"Girl, what in the world are you thanking the Lord for like that?"

"Selena, you just don't know."

"Try me."

"Girl."

"Things were getting heated, and I called?"

"How in the world did you know?"

"I came in this kitchen to turn on the stove and it popped. At first, I was just going to turn it off and not bother you, but the Spirit said, 'Call Veronica.' Of course, I tried to ignore Him, but then I smelled gas. So I said, I'd better call."

"Well, Kane was rubbing that Regina Rochelle body scrub on my feet and legs and Miss. Thang was reacting in ways I have not felt in years."

"Girl, you crazy."

"Cousin, I was about to blow a fuse. I had even prayed for an escape, and a few seconds later, you called."

"God will provide an escape."

"I'm a witness, honey."

"Look, always put this knob right here." Veronica pointed at the middle button imprinted on the back of the stove. Then, hit Oven, and it turned on without any problems.

"Okay, I got it," Selena shook her head, "and thanks for allowing me to be your escape." She giggled.

"You crazy. But I sure do thank you. I promise, I'm trying to keep myself from temptation, but it's not working. Why does God give us all this longing and passion for the opposite sex and then doesn't want us fornicating?"

"I believe fornication is deeper than we think."

"Like how?"

"Like, are you sure you want me to tell you? Me, the gold-digger who used her body to get the coins as often as I could."

"You're definitely not the same person you used to be. Girl, I see you worshiping at church, and your worship is for real. And now you have all that money you got from Rufus' safe and policies, and you still barely go shopping."

"I just realize what I desire money can't buy. As soon as I sell Rufus' home, I'm giving his mother the money and I'm buying me a home. That's if you still want me near you."

"Oh, cousin! You just don't know how happy that makes me. I wouldn't want you to do anything differently."

"Thanks, Vee. I love Bubbee, but it's good to have what feels like a sister."

"I know, right? I feel the same way about you. But back to what you said because anyone as experienced as you can teach me and any other young lady something."

"Thanks for saying that, Vee. So here it goes. I believe that what we view as fornication is what God meant to validate the marital vow. See, when he placed Adam and Eve in the garden, God didn't give them a

3

nuptial ceremony. He simply gave Adam the intellectual properties of who Eve was to be to him, and he also allowed him the relational knowledge that she came from him. So, I believe Adam knew exactly what to do to satisfy her and Eve likewise, but it wasn't about satisfaction alone. It was about the covenant of marriage. It was about oneness. Like the Oneness of God, the Father, Son, and Holy Spirit. The oneness of man, woman, and the Holy Spirit—making sure that one sperm housed in heaven would reach the opening so they could procreate."

"That's deep, Selena."

"I know, and God is showing me so much."

"So, if I got it correct. When we have sex, we basically are married."

"Exactly."

"So, that's what He meant when He told the woman at the well, you've had five husbands, and the one you have now is not your own."

"You've got it, Vee. God, just put her sexual experiences on blast, and showed her and us that it's possible to have multiple spouses that you never took to the altar, but to your bed."

"Girl, this stuff will teach. Like, Selena, no one ever tells us this in church."

"I know, right. I think some don't understand it deep enough to teach it. It's like all my life, God has been trying to show me stuff, but I try my best to ignore Him."

"Why?"

"Because Vee, to whom much is given, much is required. I don't want to be her...the woman He gives divine wisdom and knowledge to. Then I have to fight with men who don't believe I should carry His message and women who won't embrace it."

"If you asked me, I'd say forget all of them. Just be the carrier and watch God move."

"I think I'm just trying to make sure that I don't make the wrong decision again. Even when it comes to Christ. I want to have a pure heart."

"Selena, you already do. I'm so proud of you, and I just think you're going to be a blessing at Faith Temple."

"Ahh, cousin. Well, are you hungry?"

"I sure am. What were you getting ready to cook?"

Selena smirked, "Enchiladas."

"My favorite. Bring it on then. And I guess I'll call Kane over to grab a plate. He might still be hungry since tonight was our sandwich night."

"Fine, as long as you don't take them." Selena laughed, and Veronica joined her.

CHAPTER 2

K ane rose from the sofa, adjusting his pants, then stretching to relieve some of the tension he was feeling. He also knew that had it not been for Vance's little ordeal, he'd be a married man. All of his plans to marry his beloved Veronica had flown out of the window.

Instead, their family celebrated a wedding, but not his. Jasmine, his sister, and Vance, Veronica's brother, were happily married and living in her home.

The good news was Vance was picked up by the Seahawks. The bad thing—he had a series of medical visits and physical therapy and wouldn't be cleared for the league until he was at least ninety-eight-point-nine percent better.

It had been disappointing, but Kane had sense enough to know that nothing just happens.

He picked up the Regina Rochelle body scrub, screwed on the top, and took it back to his dresser. He couldn't wait until the day he could rub his wife instead of his girlfriend. *Who at my age is still calling a woman his girlfriend?*

Sure, he'd met a lot of guys in the attorney field who were old and still flaunting around girlfriends, but it wasn't a good look to him, and neither was it praiseworthy. A certain aged man, stuck from going through and scared to get married. In times like these—to Kane—he should be even more afraid to give his body to a woman who wasn't totally committed.

But then again, men who always thought they were too smart often discovered they made dumb moves.

He was an attorney who had dealt with his share of family law cases, and it still tickled him how some of the husbands who really thought they were smart, were so stupid. They'd come marching into his office like they had one-upped their wives and then find out she had pictures and proof. And then there were those who'd been in long-term-relationships with women in states which viewed common-law as serious as marriage. She stood to gain just as much, so Kane figured you might as well be married. If the looks on some of the mens faces could kill. They would.

Especially on the faces of those men who thought they were protecting themselves and their assets by not marrying, but soon found out women's rights went beyond being about to cook and work. Jilted women had ways of making you pay. Trophy pieces that turn disastrous.

Kane figured he'd rather have a wife than a trophy-piece who will leave you and aim for someone higher than you once they are gone.

He picked up his phone and dialed his mother's number.

Ring. Ring. Ring.

"You've reached the phone of Jessica Booth. Would you please leave—"

Kane hung up.

He hated leaving messages on his mother's phone because he knew it would take her four days or more to reply. Instead, he dialed someone he knew would be close to her or knew where she was.

"Hello," the deep voice answered.

"Hey, Dad. Where's Mom?"

"Boy, you think your mother in my back pocket?"

"Man, just give Moms the phone." Kane laughed. Because anytime his dad said something like that, he knew his mom was somewhere near.

"Hello, my sweet oldest son. How are you?"

"I'm straight, Mom. Look, I was just thinking. When could we get this wedding done?"

"What's wrong? Testosterone levels too high?"

"Really, Mom?"

"Who y'all think you're fooling? We were young once, and I know how things work. Can't even hardly have a light conversation with J.J. because he and Jade stay in bed."

"Moms, that's TMI. Too much information."

"I'm just saying. And poor Kane. Jasmine just flew in like Supergirl and snatched your special day right from under you."

Kane laughed. "Exactly. She's still Jasmine."

"Who are you telling?"

"Mom, you know I thought about doing just like Vance and Jasmine. Call in someone to come marry us quick."

"Boy, no! I cannot handle another shotgun nuptial. I wanted Jasper to walk our only daughter down the aisle, and that girl wasn't thinking about us. She and Vance with that hospital wedding like to have taken me out."

"But after almost losing him, Mom, that girl did what anyone in her shoes would've done."

"I guess, but I still say we can't have you following in her footsteps."

"I know. You want your children to have the most elaborate weddings so the town can brag."

"You're doggone right, and I do not deny it. With that said, I've already been working on something for you and Veronica, and I'm moving low-key."

"Lady, what do you know about low-key?"

"Boy, just because I'm your momma doesn't mean I don't have street creds. You must've forgotten I hang out at the youth center, and the youngsters keep me in there."

"I think I need to talk to my siblings to find you another pastime. Not sure if I'm digging hip mom."

"Boy, do you think I care about what you digging? I wish y'all would try to tell me where I can and can't go. I bring the rules to the Booth-Jackson school. Don't forget that."

"Oh my, now she's gone from slang to hiphop. Put Dad on the phone." Kane laughed as Jessica put the phone on speaker.

"Nawl, son, you wanted your Momma."

"Dad, that woman needs to be stopped. All I called to tell her was that I needed her to get going on my wedding."

"And she went deep in your business. Quick."

"You heard her. But she knows her boy. Man, I'm tripping over here, but we'll have to talk about it later, Pops."

"Don't try to weed me out. I know your little mannish tail about to explode. But you better take notes because sometimes going over that edge can do more harm than it helps. Maybe God is teaching you both about self-control."

"Mom, if He teaches me too much longer, I'm going to be testifying how I had to repent. I can hardly hold that woman's hands, and I'm beginning to feel like that teenage boy who didn't know what the heck his body was going to do."

"Son, just put on some of those tight undies," Jasper chimed in.

"Really, Jasper. That's your only advice. Tighty-whities. Boy, you better stop calling Veronica to your house alone. You better start inviting J.J. and Jade to dinner with you guys. Or better yet, bring her here for dinner. Sexual tension will drive you insane if you don't learn how to curb your desires."

"I know, right."

"Heck, yeah. And your poor daddy was a mess himself. He can't help you because I can barely touch him on his arms, and he inflates. So, if we've been married over thirty years and he's still having trouble keeping himself pinned down, how the world is he going to help you."

"Now, Jessica, I thought we kept our business to ourselves. You didn't have to call me out like that." They all laughed.

"Jasper, please. These boys are talking about you all the time. How you have no self-control when it comes to me. Baby, that's a good thing. It's teaching them if they do right, they'll be happily married for a long time."

"That part," Kane interjected. "Well, you good ole folks, I love y'all and, Mom, for real, get on it. I don't know how much more I can take."

"I got you, Kane. Give me a couple days to pray about the direction, and I will call you with a plan, and you can tell me what day."

"Perfect. I'll be by the house tomorrow, and we're having dinner with you all."

Jessica smiled. "Good son. And I'll call up the gang so everyone can over."

"That's a plan. Love you both and I'll see you then."

"Talk to you then, son," Jasper said before ending the call.

KANE LAUGHED AT HIS MOTHER, but she was right. He was about to lose his mind and every ounce of self-control he had. Cold shower, he was on his way. Yet again.

CHAPTER 3

Crawl sat on his sofa with his hand clutched together. Still dealing with all types of emotions, he ran his hands over his curly fade. It had been days since he'd combed his hair, but a combination of natural curls from his mother and thickness from his father still gave him the appearance of having it together. If only he felt the same.

Going undercover was beginning to get the best of him. Even after the death of Rufus, Chief still didn't want him to blow the gig. He was sure there were still wolves amongst sheep, and until every dirty cop was right where the others were, he was still Crawl—the thug attached to Rufus Burns.

Crawl, whose real name was Damon James, grew up in the streets of Dade County, and just like Rufus, had attended school with Veronica and her brother. He'd always longed to be an officer of the law, but his father convinced him that he'd make more money as an undercover agent.

His father was correct.

He made three times what regular-clothed officers made, but his job often took a toll on his mind and emotions. Sometimes he didn't even know who he was. In his line of work, you had to design an alter ego that was typically the opposite of who you were. So in the process of neglecting himself, his love life took the most significant hit. But, he was a lieutenant and was only four years away from becoming a Chief.

For the sake of the assignment, you got to know plenty of women, especially those who had a bad boy fetish. But most of them only wanted coins and sex and in that order. What Damon couldn't understand is how beautiful women like Selena got hooked up with criminals like Rufus.

In some ways, he could see why. Selena was always dressed to the nines, but so was Rufus. Damon could even see how he'd probably won her heart with money and stuff, but he refused to label her as a gold digger. And Rufus did have more than money. He was brilliant, which is why Damon never in a million years, would've thought Rufus would commit suicide. But sometimes you misread things and people.

This time, he ran his hand over his face.

Then Damon folded his lips in. There was something still bothering him, deeply, or rather someone. He still couldn't shake the fear he saw in Selena's eyes that morning. She looked at him as if she saw a ghost. And although he'd come to ask her some questions, her beautiful eyes full of fear changed his mind.

Damon never wanted to hurt her or cause her any unnecessary pain. And the look—straight terror—was something he would never want her to feel towards him. But had he known she was making moves like she was, he would have given her his number and told her everything.

She deserved to know.

How he had kept her safe. Even how he threatened Rufus about choking her. His mind drifted...

"Dude, you think it's cool you sitting here harping on how you choked your wife?"

"You said it, my wife, and I can say whatever I want to say."

"Rufus, this your gig, but don't play with me. And if you ever come up in here bragging about how you choked her, I'll choke you." He stood from his chair just as Rufus stood.

If it was one thing Crawl had on the streets, it was pure respect, and when

Rufus stood, the others stood, but behind Crawl. And that was all he needed to know he was doing right by them.

He'd known that it was Rufus who so-called ran the show, but Crawl was the man. It was what his mother told him that worked for his life— always be kind to people, share your substance with them, help them without boasting, turning your back on them when they are down is a no, and son if you do these things, people will always be for you.

Her words had proven to be true. Damon did just what Rufus had never attempted to do...take care of them. His protection became so valid, he even warned them against criminal activities, and they obeyed him. Damon bought diapers, food, and had also paid rent. Then he bought a car detail shop to put twenty of them to legal work.

Although he was undercover, he'd known God had a plan for his life, which included him being the *Good American*.

Damon's mind was still on Selena. Rufus mistreated her. He often took his mind off of battering her by talking about money or something that meant more to Rufus. Damon didn't know if she'd noticed, but that was the least he could do. Then, he didn't want to do too much, either. Exposing himself was much more than his willingness to protect her.

Damon's mind drifted to D2. He'd tried to keep him from being so invested, but D2 was Rufus' boy to his heart. "He would have sold me out quick," Damon mumbled.

But now he's twelve feet under.

Damon felt wholeheartedly Rufus killed him, but he had no proof. Even when he distracted D2 at the stadium from grabbing Veronica, that was all apart of his plan. But yet, Rufus had dealt dangerously with D2 but never once even called him. "Maybe God was really on his side because if Rufus had even acted like he wanted to run on my feet, I would have had to deal with him."

Damon shook his head.

One thing was for sure: as soon as this case was completely over, he was going to get Selena. Even if it meant leaving the force. She deserved to be loved. Cherished. All of the things she ever wanted or needed would be for him to do.

CHAPTER 4

Selena cleaned the kitchen and laughed so hard at Veronica until tears began flowing down her cheeks. When he came to get the food, she acted as though she was dropping a hot potato in his hand. The chemistry between the two of them was comical but cute. But Selena understood perfectly well what Veronica was running from.

She only wished she would have been so smart when it came to Rufus. Loving him had been easy, especially when she felt she was one-upping her cousin. And all the feelings of hatred towards Veronica and their family had flown away.

All the years she'd been fooled into thinking it was Aunt Valerie who abandoned them, she realized it was they who'd left her. A family could be stressful on so many different levels, but it was downright traumatic when they thought they could run your life.

Now she and her cousin were where they should have been all their lives. Together. They were bonding and growing together as women and in Christ. At least so much was behind them, and the best was yet to come. She just wished she was completely done with everything.

One of the hardest tasks of her life was before her. Selena had to go back to Dade to plan the funeral of the husband who never loved her. It did cross her mind to cremate him, but only because of his mother, she had compassion. Ms. Burns had already taken a hard hit when her beloved Rufus shot himself, not to mention that he was her most significant income source. Her SSI check would have never afforded her the type of life she lived. But Selena had taken even that into consideration.

Because of her turning over state's evidence, she still got Rufus's six hundred thousand dollar police policy. Through this provision—an officer taking his life because of distress—it also made her million-dollar policy effective. But God did even greater. There was the one-point-two million she got for the sale of his lakefront property, the five hundred thousand from the east side property, which she paid off Ms. Burns home with and gave her the two hundred and thirty-thousand left, and the three million in stocks and bonds.

Selena donated five hundred thousand of that to *Change*—a non-profit for battered women who needed, wanted, and desired change. She gave his mother an additional five hundred thousand since SSI took her check because of the first two hundred and thirty-thousand, and the rest, she deposited it into her checking account.

Now, she had more money than she'd ever dreamt of having and didn't want to spend a dime. There was something life-changing about Louisiana. She came here escaping life with Rufus but had, in return, discovered a deeper life in Christ.

Selena dried the dishes and went to find her cousin.

"Knock. Knock," Selena said as she also included two physical knocks.

"Come in, Selena." Veronica smiled and patted her bed as an invitation for Selena to sit.

"Thanks, cousin. I really hate to bother you, but..." Selena held her hands in prayer position, then continued, "I need you."

"What's going on?"

"As you know, I have to bury Rufus this weekend."

"Yes, and how's that coming?"

"I've done all I can to keep the memorial short and as sweet as it can be given who Rufus was. But I really need someone with me."

"You got it."

"Are you sure? Given your history with him."

"He was once upon a time my best friend; the guy I thought the sun and stars rose because of. But hey, he was my cousin's husband." Veronica laughed and touched Selena's hand.

"Well, that's settled."

Veronica could see the tension in Selena's facial expression. "To be honest, Selena, Rufus wasn't always a bad guy. I cannot bear the weight of not forgiving him, and neither can you. This will be an opportunity for my family and me, including you, to move on."

"I realized that especially when Pastor Strong preached Forgiving is for the Forgiver. I knew I had to forgive, but I also knew what I had to do concerning his mother."

"Ms. Burns," Veronica shook her head, "an absolute jewel. She deserved a son who did right, but she got the exact opposite."

"I know, right?" Selena swiped a tear.

"Yeah, so sad."

"My heart just goes out to her because he was her only child. I've taken care of her financially, but I'm never going to leave her alone. I promised to be the daughter she never had, and so with, and now without, Rufus, I'm still going to uphold my promise."

"Selena, I love you, and I'm so proud of you."

"Well, since you've designed my dream home, I'm thinking of asking her to come to live here with me. I just believe this is what the Lord wants from me."

"A real twentieth-century Naomi and Ruth."

"Girl, I wouldn't call it all that. Just knowing how lonely life gets when you're alone and trying to keep her from feeling that type of pain."

"I think it's a great idea, Selena. And I'll even help you with her. She's so special to me too."

"Well, I'm going to hold you to that, and I know she'll love the four-bedroom mother's home you created. It's right by the pool, and that woman loves swimming and fishing. And since Cross Lake is a part of our backyard, I'm sure she'll be in house heaven." Selena laughed, and Veronica joined in with her.

"Well, cousin, I'm glad we've gotten that straightened out. Now, if only I can talk this tension out of my body, so I can enjoy being with the man I love."

"It'll get better. Sometimes God will allow things like what you are experiencing to happen, so you'll know what you're missing. Self-control."

"I can see that, because I found out tonight mine is fleeting."

"Well, now you need to figure out how long you can be around him without losing it, and what's the new limitation standards. Like tonight, you found out rubbing your feet and legs is a no-no."

"Girl, who would have ever thought I couldn't take a foot rub?"

"Veronica, our bodies react to what's in his touch. So nine times out of ten, Kane is going through exactly what you are if not ten times worse."

"His can't be bad as mine."

"Girl, please. Some women would have never had sex if it weren't for a man having it worse than them. I believe God made it that way. He made us be passive bystanders, but with slight feelings of longing. But them. It's drastic. And you do know it takes a seeder to transform us into the carrier?"

"Why dang, Selena. You've thought about this on such a deep level."

"I have because, to be honest, I had to evaluate why I had sex with anyone I had sex with. My first was a complete idiot, and then Rufus, a mess. So, I had to figure out what drew me to them so I won't repeat the cycle."

"Well, I understand that perfectly. I guess I've seen so many women in the same situation—giving themselves to men who never loved them —and then they are left with all the emotional baggage. I never want that."

Selena stood up. "I don't think anyone does. I just believe we women get to a point where we have sexual desires too. I just think we some-times give in not because of our desires, but because we feel needed by them. Which, in turn, makes us feel special. But after it's over, we feel guilt, and they feel accomplished."

"Wow. I really never saw it like that."

"Yeah, they are accomplished because if it does what it was meant to do—plant seed—they are doing exactly what God wanted them to do. And often, if we get the seed of a man who doesn't love us, we feel so used, but then the love of that child becomes enough for us to somewhat get over it. But then again, some women give them natural trouble in every area she can find to give it. He planted his seed there, but didn't love her or the seed enough to stay there. Life is crazy."

"No, it's just simple when we put God in every aspect. This is exactly why I'm putting ice between these legs and knees until Kane makes me his wife. I declare and decree I will not fall prey to my flesh, in Jesus' name."

"Amen," they both said.

CHAPTER 5

K ane woke up, put his hands behind his head, and peered at the ceiling. He felt terrible Veronica even needed an escape. Because surely, Selena had called her right on time. Kane was sensitive enough to the Spirit to know what had just happened. But he wished it hadn't.

He almost allowed his hands to float to places he would have never even thought of touching, in his right mind.

Kane grimaced.

"Lord, You have to hurry this wedding date up or pour some cooling aid from heaven over my flesh."

He threw the covers back and slid his legs off the side of the bed. It was time to get up and get ready for work. But before he did anything, he knew he needed to do two things. Pray. And call Veronica to apologize.

He'd owed her that much.

So, Kane kneeled beside his bed, prayed, and then picked up his phone to dial Veronica's number.

"Hello, sweetheart," Veronica answered after the second ring.

"Hey, baby. Look, I wanted to apologize."

"For what?"

"For going farther than I ever expected to go, and staying in a place in my mind longer than I needed. Veronica, I love you but I never want to disrespect you or coerce you into doing anything you're not ready to do."

"Kane, I'm just as guilty as you. I wanted you almost as bad as you wanted me, but I just don't want to pay the cost for lust. You do know sex will cost us something, right?"

"I know, Vee. But that doesn't stop the longing I feel. We've been together a little over six months, and there's not one day that I haven't envisioned waking up to you by my side. I dream of being one with you in the most intimate of ways, and I'm never ashamed because I know God created you for me. I know you are the very rib that's absent from my side. And although I never want to jeopardize what we have, I don't think I can hide what I'm feeling."

"I understand."

"So, what's the solution?"

"Why don't we stop seeing each other for a while? Maybe, until we both calm down."

Kane's voice changed. "That's your solution?"

"Kane, don't be angry."

"Vee, I'm coming to you telling you about my longing for you, and your decision is to break up?"

"I didn't say, 'break-up.' I said, 'stop seeing each other' as in stop spending so much time alone."

"So, now you feel like I'm so out-of-control we need babysitters every time we're together?"

"Kane, stop. You are going too far."

"Oh, so you didn't go too far with what you just said? Alright, later, Vee." He hung up the phone.

VERONICA LOOKED AT HER SCREEN. She knew Kane didn't just do what she thought he did. *I know this dude didn't hang up on me.* She dialed his number, and it went straight to voicemail. She dialed it three more times because it seemed as though he was forwarding her calls.

She was livid.

One mind wanted to go kick his door in, but her sane mind knew that would be too much. *Heck, I was only trying to save us both.* She put on her clothes, still fuming. It was the best she could do to keep her from going off the deep end.

And the closer she came to being finished packing, the tears flowed like a river.

She and Kane had never even disagreed before, and their first fight was damaging enough to end things forever. Who hangs up the phone in the face of someone they claim to love? That was so not good.

Veronica laid her head in her hand, and then she felt the touch of love.

Her cousin Selena was standing there, rubbing her head and wiping her tears. This was the exact moment when Veronica knew she needed Selena as much as Selena needed her. Through sniffles, she heard Selena saying, "It's going to be alright, cousin. But whatever you do, don't let the enemy get in."

"But, Selena, he so disrespected me."

"He probably just was too upset, Veronica. Would you rather Kane say something in anger he doesn't mean or just hang up the phone?"

"Neither, because I would have never done either to him. I'm good."

"No, you're not good, but you will be as soon as you forgive."

"Not happening. I'm going to tie up some loose ends at the office, and we can leave for Dade tonight. I need some time away and maybe, Kane does too. Please pack your bags, and I'll make our flight arrangements while I'm at the job."

"Okay, but—"

"No buts, Selena."

"Okay, Vee. I'll be ready, or I can just meet you at the airport."

"No, I'll come back home. I have a packed bag in the closet, but I'd like to add some things I bought for Abuela."

"Okay. I'll be ready, and please drive careful.

"I will, and thanks."

"For what? Cleaning your snotty nose?"

Veronica laughed. "You know you're crazy, right?"

"Girl, it's a family trait, I see." Selena hugged Veronica and handed her the car keys from the table.

⚜

KANE THREW HIS PHONE, causing it to shatter against the wall. It was best he ended the call when he did. Kane was about to tell her something he wouldn't be able to apologize for.

He went into the bathroom to get in the shower.

You know you went too far. Call Veronica and apologize.

Kane mumbled, "I can't if I wanted to. I just broke my phone."

Kane decided when he finished dressing, he would stop by her place to apologize. He was wrong for not giving her time to explain herself, but she had suggested the absolute wrong decision, which set him off.

Kane put on his Tom Ford micro-check dress shirt, and then pulled on the trousers to his three-piece Herringbone Solaro navy suit. He looked in his mirror as he brushed his thick wavy black hair and applied the Regina Rochelle beard balm to his neatly cut and lined beard.

Afterward, he put his contacts in because his suit was too clean to wear glasses today. He had a briefing in Judge Sims' courtroom, and he had to represent the men of law and his clients in a way that was conducive to integrity, honesty, loyalty, and compassion.

After he gave himself the nod of approval, he retrieved his red with white dots Giorgio Armani tie, put it on, as well as his vest and buttoned it up. This morning he would keep his jacket on the hanger in his car until it was time for him to get out.

He was on point. His deposition was straight.

And he was ready to get another day behind him but not before taking care of Veronica and making sure that everything between them was okay.

Well, he actually wanted it to be better than okay, but okay would suffice better than it was when he'd hung up the phone. *In her face.*

He cringed because he couldn't believe he'd done that. Just the thought of Veronica making the decision to end their relationship because they were both horny was absolutely heartbreaking to him. *How could she possibly think that would be the right decision?* Kane grabbed his briefcase and made a mental note to go by the cell phone store.

He opened his door, closed and locked it, and then took a deep breath before knocking on Veronica's door.

"Who is it," he heard Selena ask.

"Me, Kane."

Selena swung the door open.

"What do you want, Mr. Rude?"

"Selena, good morning. Is she here?"

"She's gone, and if you don't make this right, it may be for good."

"Thank you, Selena. I'll fix this, I promise." Kane turned and swiftly walked out of the building.

CHAPTER 6

Jessica could feel something going on in the atmosphere. Sort of the same feelings she'd gotten whenever they were into something they shouldn't be or had done something wrong. She tried to turn her attention back to Valerie and the ladies she entertained to move the wedding date closer.

It took a minute to gather herself, but it also took excusing herself from the room.

Jessica dialed Jasmine's phone.

"Hello, sweet, Mother," Jasmine answered on the first ring.

"Hello, my sweet baby girl. How are you and Vance?"

"Mom, everything is good. Vance is almost at the ninety-eight percent the doctor needed him to be. He's working so hard, Mom. I just pray he doesn't do too much."

"Girl, he's a man. He'll never do too much unless he tries to put himself on a cross to die like Jesus. Anything else is nothing because God put His breath and the strength of His Word in him."

"Girl, you are the best. I'm so proud to have you, Mom."

"Young lady, I'm the proud one. So, give Vance my love, and I will chat with you as soon as I get the definite date for Kane and Veronica's wedding."

"Okay, love. Please don't overdo it. I love you."

"I love you, too, Jasmine." Jessica hung up the phone.

She quickly dialed Kane's number, and it went straight to his voicemail.

"Kane, this is your mother. Call me as soon as you can. I need to see how you are. Is something going on? I love you and call me."

Jessica hung up and dialed J.J's number.

"Hey, lady," he answered on the third ring.

"Hey to you, young man. How are you and Jade?"

"Mom, we're good. I know you felt something, huh?"

"Boy, you don't know me that well."

"I bet I do. And I bet you've called all three of us. The only one you haven't spoken to is Kane."

"What has Kane done?"

"Momma, you want to hear it from the ignorant horse's mouth."

"First of all, don't call your brother ignorant or my child a horse. Now, what did he do."

"First, he hung the phone up on Veronica. Then the nut threw a thousand-dollar-phone. Now, he has no woman or a phone. He went to get a phone, but it will take three days before it comes in. Just crazy."

"I knew one of you were into something. Where's your brother now?"

"He's in court. As soon as he gets back, I'll tell knucklehead to call you."

"Son, stop acting and thank you." Jessica gasped.

"Mom, you mustn't worry about him. He's going to do what he needs to do."

"I wish it were that easy, son, now let me get back to the meeting."

"Love you, Mom."

"I love you more, J.J."

After their confessions of love, Jessica hung up and then dialed Veronica, grunting when her phone went straight to voicemail. She waited to leave a message, "Ronica, this is Momma J., call me as soon as you can. Love you, sweetheart." Jessica ended the call and walked back to the table where Valerie, First Lady Destiny Strong, the sisters Jamecia and Jayla, and Priscilla and Regina awaited her.

"Is everything okay?" Valerie leaned in and asked.

"Not sure what it is, Val, but something's going on with Kane and Veronica. I don't have the full details because I couldn't get her or Kane. Let's just pray."

Valerie touched Jessica's hand. "I'll whisper a word of prayer."

"Ladies, thank you all so very much for allowing me a moment to check on my family. I don't know too much more than I did when I left, but what I do know is God has those three and their mates. I've kept them before the Lord, and He's promised to take care of them."

"Mrs. Booth, we know God will take care of them. If you need anything from us, please don't hesitate to reach out to me or Pastor Strong." First Lady Destiny smiled and patted Jessica on the hand.

"Thank you, First Lady. All we can do is trust God. When they were children, I learned if God is going to take care of them, I needed to move out of the way. I just remind Him sometimes of His promise to keep me and mine. And it works."

"Hallelujah, He will do it," Valerie yelled.

Most of them laughed, but all of them knew her son, Vance, had escaped death because of a faithful God. She understood much more than anyone at the table how God will take care of your child even when you couldn't do a thing.

Valerie cried as she spoke, "Our children already face so much because of their skin, but the devil just targets them on all types of angles and levels."

Jessica nodded, knowing full well what Valerie meant, "But blessed be unto the God who created and controls, and may He protect them when we, their mothers, cannot."

"Sometimes, I ask God what made me so special that He didn't let Vance become another senselessly murdered victim. And all I know is it was His grace." Valerie threw her hands in the air.

Now, they all cried.

Jessica wiped her eyes. "We are seven black women who all have one thing in common. We all desire God's protection for our children. Our families. In a world filled with so much hatred towards black men and women, and so much hopelessness in our black communities, we need God."

"And it's not just about our children anymore. Our hearts hurt for all the mothers around the world who have to pray for God's protection daily. I'm thanking God it wasn't me who had to bury my son or daughter, but at the same time I'm hurting and crying as if Sandra Bland or even George Floyd were my own." Destiny shook her head as emotions gripped them all.

"As mothers, sisters in Christ, when one of us hurts, we all hurt. I don't care if the world sees my pain as a black woman, I just want justice. I want the world to see our pain. How we feel to watch a mother's son die at the hands of the police. How we hurt as if it were our own child." Priscilla slammed her hand on the table.

"This is why I almost didn't marry Jacob. Like black children have enough troubles but to have mixed babies. Lord, I can't hardly imagine how mad I'd be if you even looked at my babies in a strange way." Jamecia dabbed her eyes.

"Jamecia, we all belong to God. And the deepest expression of love comes when we see one another as God's creation instead of as black or white. You and your babies will be fine, and we promise, we will pray for them as much as we pray for our own." Jessica stretched her arm around Jamecia.

"I will admit, though, the heaviness of mothering a black child goes much deeper than getting them fed and through keeping them from being murdered by careless, mean, and proud racists—hidden behind sheep's outfits—white men. Or even by reckless, hopeless, and hateful black men with guns, or women who couldn't let go of the infatuation of relationships, as my son endured. Yet we mustn't regret who we love or why we love. It's of God and love is always right," Valerie finished speaking and reached behind Jessica to pat Jasmine's back.

"Amen," they all chimed in.

"We are seven black mothers grappling with the pain felt by the mothers who have lost their babies to unjustified murder, senseless crimes, racially targeted situations, or cancer and the silent diseases. We hurt, but not as those who begin to second guess our choices, hate, or embrace hopelessness. We have a God who created the Heavens and the earth and knew everything before He placed our children in our wombs. He knew who would become a martyr and whose name would be known by the world." Jessica wiped her tears. "And, He is still on the throne, so why don't we meet Him there?"

"Amen," they exclaimed and bowed.

"Lord, we lift up every mother in this world who feels like we feel right now. Please protect our babies and keep them from evil. Lord, allow those who have lost their babies to be the picture of strength that we need to heal. Cause us all to understand You will repay, vindicate, and take care of Your own, in Jesus' name. Amen."

"Amen," they all said as they each got up from their seats and gathered together to hold one another.

CHAPTER 7

Veronica rushed back to the house and finished packing her bags. Selena told her that Kane came by, which was even more reason for them to hurry. At this point, she didn't want to see nor talk to Kane. When would she feel different? Only God knew. They needed separation, not in the wrong way, but he'd made it that way. Since he had no need to listen to her explanation, it would remain that way until she felt better.

"Are you ready, Selena?"

"I am. Are you sure you don't want to go by Kane's office before we leave?"

"I'm sure, and please don't mention him again."

"Okay, but I am not in agreement with the way you're leaving."

"You don't have to be, Selena. I'm just trying to do this the way I think is best. Kane disrespected and disgraced me. I would've never done him like that, but it came so easy for him. Now, he's going to learn a lesson early, and if he never learns it, then it's not meant to be."

"I won't say anything else, but you cannot stop me from praying."

"Deal. Now let's go. I can't wait to see Lita. I know she's going to be excited to see us too."

"I know she is, and she's going to think you're absolutely too skinny."

"That's not funny." Veronica hit Selena.

"Ouch, that hurt."

"I'm glad."

"Come on, girl. Are you trying to let Kane catch us here."

"No, but should I?"

"Not."

"Well, let's go then." Selena pulled her cousin by the arm, and after Veronica set the house, they left.

⚜

KANE FINISHED HIS DEPOSITION. After court adjourned, he gathered his belongings and left. He looked around, trying to see if he saw his secretary, but she was gone. Hope must've dashed out as soon as the judge dismissed them.

He couldn't be mad because he would have done the exact same thing.

Kane picked up his briefcase and headed for the elevator. He needed to make things right with Veronica. After thinking about the conversation over and over in his head, he surmised he was so wrong. Kane spotted one of his old classmates, Chuck Waters, and asked to use his cellphone.

"J.J., have you heard from Veronica?"

"Man, nawl, and what you doing with Chuck's phone?"

"He's here at the courthouse. I borrowed it. I'm on my way to the office."

"Good, because I went to the Orange Store and got you a real cell phone and canceled that mess you were willing to wait three days for."

"Man, I love you."

"I'm going to see if you still love me after you talk to Jessica Booth." J.J. laughed.

"J.J., what did you tell Mom?"

"That her ignorant son done the fool and now doesn't have a woman."

"You didn't?"

"You shouldn't have made me."

Kane hung up in his brother's face.

This hanging up thing was becoming a bit too comfortable. Too much for one day. But J.J. had no right to tell their mother anything. He would have covered for J.J., but no, he had to open his big mouth.

Kane opened the door to his car, took off his jacket, hung it on the hanger, and put it on the hook in his vehicle. Then he jumped in his car, slamming the door. His first mind said, *go to Veronica's*, but Kane thought better of it. He decided he'd try to get her on the phone first, so he went straight to the office.

As soon as he opened the door to his office, his mother swirled around in his chair.

"Kane Jackson Booth, what have you done?"

"Mom, I promise I didn't do anything but hang up the phone in Veronica's face. At least I couldn't slam it like you used to do in my and J.J.'s face when we were young."

"Boy, I am your mother, and Vee is not your child. You had no right hanging up on her, and now you will suffer the consequences of your decision. When you decided to hang up in her face, you made the wrong decision, and now she's gone."

"What do you mean she's gone?"

"She flew to Dade today."

"Mom, you have to be kidding me."

"I'm serious and do not go there. You need to give Vee time to think and forgive you. But as long as you live, you better not ever disrespect her like that again. Kane, to get so angry that you hang up on the woman you love, says you didn't care about her feelings at all. And if she never talks to you again, it will be your fault."

J.J. walked into the office.

"Man, what is it with these women we chose? They get mad and run to Florida."

"J.J., I never thought about that." Jessica laughed.

"This is not a laughing matter," Kane shouted.

"Boy, I will slap spit from your lips. Who you think you're talking to.

Have you lost your ever-loving-rabbit-behind mind?" Jessica shot him a look that made him humble down.

"No, Ma'am. I'm sorry, Mom. I'm just stressed. How could she leave without telling me?"

"Easy, or the same way you hung up in her face," Jessica retorted. "Now, if you ask me, you are now reaping exactly what you sowed. What's funny is a grown man would allow himself to get so mad that he stops talking, and have the nerves to think she was supposed to talk to you about making a move! It's funny because if you don't get your stuff together, you'll be standing at the front of that venue alone."

"I'll be just like my knucklehead brother waiting four years until she returns home."

"Oh, so we ragging now?" J.J. asked.

"I am and J.J. you deserve anything I give you right now."

"Rag on, but if you know like I know, you'll be somewhere praying. Veronica is a beauty, and those full lips are enough to drive any man insane."

"Don't play with me, J.J."

Jessica jumped in. "Alright, alright. I'm still in this room, and I will slap the taste out of both of your mouths. Now, where is the wedding book? I didn't see it on the table when I came in."

Kane mashed the intercom, "Hope."

"Yes, Sir."

"Would you bring that book you did in here of J.J's wedding?"

"I'm on my way."

Hope knocked twice and entered after she heard Jessica say, "Come in."

"Here you are, Mrs. Booth."

"Thank you, Hope," Jessica reached for the beautifully decorated photo book. And Hope turned to leave.

"Wait, Hope. Who did this?"

"My sister-in-law owns Country Girl Creations, and she designs all sorts of things."

"Well, you tell your sister that I will need another one just like this if this knucklehead does something useful with himself."

"Yes, Ma'am." Hope laughed as she left Kane's office. Mrs. Booth always amused her, and she often wondered if she'd ever be that authoritative with her family. But first, she had to get a man.

"Mom, did you have to say that in front of Hope?"

"Boy, that girl isn't thinking about you. That's why I love her. But, I know the perfect person for Ms. Hope."

"There you go with that matchmaking stuff." J.J. grabbed his mother.

"Well, and Selena is too mature for Austin Davenport, but I think Hope would be perfect for him."

"Mom, I think you have something," J.J. said, fist-bumping her.

Jessica furrowed her eyebrows. "Boy, you think…"

CHAPTER 8

Selena pulled up to Abuela's house and touched Veronica on her
shoulder.

"We're here, cousin."

"I must be tired."

"You were snoring before we even pulled off the parking lot good.
Chief Linnear had us escorted to Marita's house, so I guess we will stay
here tonight." Selena called their grandmother by her name, not
wanting to offend Veronica.

"Sounds good to me."

They got out of the car and got only one of their bags a piece. And
whoever it was in the cop car was parked across the street from their
Abuela's house waiting on them to go inside. After they got in, Selena
turned to wave at the cop, but he didn't move. She immediately dialed
Chief Linnear.

"Chief Linnear, we are in the house now, but the cop didn't leave."

"He's not going to leave, Selena. We are going to have the same cop
assigned to you until you leave here. He's going to be in plain clothes
because I don't trust anyone but him to look after you."

"Okay, who is he?"

"His name is Damon James, but Rufus and the streets call him Crawl."

"Crawl. The Crawl that was best buds with Rufus. The one who came to my house the day I left and scared me stupid."

"Yes. Him. He's an undercover agent but no one here knows that—only you. So don't tell anyone. Not even your Abuela."

"Okay, I won't. But that's crazy."

"Mi hermosa nietas (My beautiful granddaughters)." Their abuela raced to them with big hugs.

"I'll tell you about it later," Selena said to Veronica as they raced to meet her.

"Estoy muy feliz de verlos a los dos (I'm so happy to see you both)," Marita Verez Elnunez hugged them so hard.

"And, Veronica, estoy tan feliz de tenerte en mi vida (I'm so happy to have you in my life.)"

"Gracias, Abuela (thank you, grandmother)," Veronica a little hesitant, kissed Marita on the cheek.

"Ven deja que te lleve a tu habitación (Come let me take you to your room)." Marita took the girls by their arms and guided them to the most beautiful room. One she had specially made for her granddaughters, and it was filled with pictures of both Veronica and Selena. They were the only two girls.

"Gracias, Abuela (thank you, grandmother)," Selena said as she led Veronica around the room looking at their pictures.

"Les cocine algo de comida chicas (I cooked you girls some food)," Marita said and gestured for the girls to come on.

This time Selena spoke, "Danos un minuto, Abuela, y estaremos allí (give us a minute, Grandmother, and we will be right there)."

Marita said as she turned to leave, "Bien, te estaré esperando a ustedes dos chicas (okay, I will be waiting for you, two girls)."

It was Veronica's time to reply, "Bien, Abuela (okay, grandmother)."

As soon as Marita closed the door, Selena grabbed her bag to change into something more comfortable, and Veronica replaced her heels with slippers.

"Vee, do you remember me telling you about the Crawl guy?"

"Yes, I remember. The one you said there was something about. The one who went to school with you and Vance?"

"Yes, him. I told you it was almost like he was protecting me from Rufus sometimes."

"Yes, and…"

"Chief Linnear just told me he was an undercover cop. He also said I couldn't tell anyone, including Grandmother. Vee, what the heck was going on?"

"You said he would look at you some sort of way. Maybe, he was trying to assure you that you were alright."

"Vee, I thought something was wrong with me. Because at one point, I was thinking I was catching feelings. You just don't know how many times Rufus would have beat me silly if it wasn't for him. And then one night, he accused me of having Crawl because he always came to my rescue. I promise, at that point, I hadn't even noticed him. He's good looking, but I didn't need Rufus' friends coming for me. So, I felt out of sight, out of mind."

"I feel you. Well, you do know how God works, and maybe He put Crawl there for you. Come to think of it, I know He put him there for me. D2 would have snatched me at that game, but Crawl made sure I saw him. It was like he was trying to let me know he was there to do something to me. The way he looked at me caused me to go in that bathroom and ask those girls to surround me."

"Girl, girl."

"God works in mysterious ways, Selena. And like you said the day you left, if he wanted you, he probably would have got you. He was probably torn about telling you the truth about who he was."

"Probably. But I'm glad Damon didn't. I would have thought he was lying and probably would have shot him myself. I was so darn scared that day, and I would have shot my way away from there."

"I know. I feel you."

"Well, come on, let's eat all this unhealthy food so you can talk to your Abuela all night, and I can fall asleep on both of you."

"Really, Selena."

"Really."

CHAPTER 9

It took everything in Kane not to call Reginald Strong for his airplane. He wanted to go after her, but he also knew how important it was for her and Selena to take care of Rufus's unfinished business.

Kane opened the files from the earlier court session and smiled. At least now, Valerie was the sole owner of all the properties in Dade County owned by her husband. They were one step closer to finalizing all things concerning Vance Sr.'s death, legacy, and estate.

Kane propped his elbows on his desk and rested his face in his hands. This had been an extremely long day. Everything he thought could go wrong between him and Veronica had. He hung up on her, but she'd also left him and gone three states away. But could he blame her? If she had hung up on him, he would have been just as livid.

The stress of the entire situation definitely weighed on him. He rotated his neck and then lifted one hand to his chin and the other to his head, stretching his neck to relieve some of the tension.

Be angry, but sin not.

How many times had he heard that? How many times had he allowed his emotions to swirl, becoming an unjustifiable hurricane? Too often. But in his defense, it took something terrible to push him into a negative act.

In reality, had Veronica never insisted on them breaking up, he would have been good. Horny, but good.

⚜

JESSICA PUT her purse on the kitchen table and went to the sink to wash her hands. She usually never washed her hands in the kitchen sink, but because of Covid-19, the closest sink—in her view—was the best sink. After she finished, she snatched a paper towel from the dispenser and dried her hands.

"Hey, girl." Jasper walked into the kitchen and straight to his wife, bending to kiss her gently.

"Hey, baby. How has your day been?"

Jasper smoothed his goatee with his hand. "It's been. What about your? Did you get anything accomplished at the meeting?"

"I did, but the strangest thing happened. Mid-meeting, I started feeling like something was going on with one of the children."

"Okay, and we both know it usually is. So, who is it now?"

"Kane and Veronica. He hung up the phone in her face and then threw his phone and broke it. You know, she probably called it over and over, and then when it kept sending her to voicemail, she figured she'd cut him by going to Dade with Selena and not telling Kane a thing."

Jasper laughed. "Oh, she pulled a Jade?"

"Exactly, and he is feeling like crap."

"Well, he's grown. He did something stupid that he's going to have to pay for. It's good Vee's showing him early that she isn't taking no stuff off him."

"And you know J.J. He drove the stake into Kane's heart. That son of yours is a complete mess, Jasper."

"He's just like his momma."

"Oh, so you say."

"Girl, it would be a crime if you didn't drive us when we did something crazy. Why you think James and I called you Indy driver of the car

46

named Pain? Because you can drive what we did so deep to make us feel the pain of our own actions."

"Good. If I didn't, you'd continue in foolishness, and I can't allow that to happen."

Jasper pulled Jessica in his arms. "Yeah, right."

Ring. Ring.

"Soon as I get ready to kiss you, that darn phone rings."

"Aw, baby, you have me all your life to kiss me when you want to. Give me a few, that's the first lady."

"Tell her hello," Jasper said as he released Jessica to answer the call.

"Hello, First Lady."

"Hello, Jessica. Tell me, did you have time to look over the designs yet?"

"Actually, I just walked in the house, took off that mask, and washed my hands. I'll be so glad when this Covid mess is controlled."

"Us too. So, you can just call me later."

"Okay, but there's something I want to ask."

"Shoot."

"You said that Dr. Rosalee Day helped you with some things?"

"Yes, she is wonderful. You know our people never seek counseling, and sometimes we deal with stuff that's been carried over from our childhood. Do you need to see her?"

"No, but I would love for Kane to visit her. You know, he's had this anger issue since the time he was a young lad. We've prayed over him, oiled him down, and came against every demon we know to cast out. But, he did something today that made me see those hidden tendencies are still there."

"I get you. Why don't you let me tell pastor to call Dr. Day, and set you up something? Do you want him to go tomorrow?"

"We'd better make it as soon as possible, so if she can get him in tomorrow, that would be fine. I'll call him to see what he's got tomorrow and what time he'll be finished. I'll call you back."

"Sounds like a plan. Talk to you soon."

Jessica hit the red button to end the call and then pressed the green

Talk button. She immediately dialed Kane's number and waited for him to answer.

"Hello, Mom, what did I do now?"

"Actually, this call is about what I didn't do. Kane, I want you to come with me tomorrow. Can I swing by the office and pick you up around nine."

"Uhum..."

"It's vital to me son."

"Sure, Mom. I'll move some things around. Will we be back by noon?"

"I believe we will, but just in case, let's do lunch. I'll have you back by one."

"Okay, lunch's on you, Mrs. Booth."

"Whatever. Bye, no, talk to you later, son."

"Love you, Mom."

That went easier than Jessica imagined it would. Now, she needed to call First Lady to make sure it was a go with Dr. Day.

Destiny answered on the third ring. "Hello, Jessica."

"Hello, sweetheart. Were you and pastor able to get Dr.Day?"

"We sure were, and she said she'll see him at the top of the morning at nine-thirty or eleven. Whichever is best for him."

"I know I was in the Spirit because I told Kane I will come to get him at nine. Just enough time for me to tell him where and why he's going and grab a bite to eat in case it takes longer than I think. Maybe, it will also give us a moment to go in together."

"Dr. Day is a jewel and very accommodating, so all you have to do is tell her what you all need. She's as kind as she is anointed."

"I heard the anointing at the Mother's Day banquet. She also seemed kind. That's what I felt when she helped some of those who were slain in the Spirit get up. I saw that much."

"Yeah, that was the best and I can't wait until next year."

"I think I'm looking forward to that as well. You did a great job, and it's going to take a lot to top that More Than Diamonds banquet."

"Well, one thing I know, it's not on me to top it...that's God's job and

His alone. I'm just glad He chose to use my mind and hands to assist Him."

"Amen. That right there is why I love me some you. Always giving God the glory."

"Jessica, I have to. He's too good to be placed second in anything. Let me know how things go tomorrow."

"I will, thanks again. And I'll talk to you tomorrow if the Lord wills."

"Same here."

CHAPTER 10

Veronica barely slept, but it wasn't because of the bed, either. The room designated for Marita's granddaughters was fit for queens. The pillow-top mattresses felt like what Veronica figured it would be like resting on clouds. She swung her legs onto the side of the bed. Selena was still asleep, so in her attempt not to wake her, she quietly grabbed her phone off the nightstand that separated their beds and tipped towards the bathroom.

As soon as she turned the knob, the door of their bedroom came open.

"Shush," she whispered. "Sleepyhead is still sleeping. I'll meet you in the kitchen as soon as I get dressed."

"Bien nieta," Marita whispered and quietly closed the door.

"Think you're gonna eat all that good breakfast without me, huh?" Selena mumbled.

Veronica laughed because if nothing else could awaken Selena, food, or just the mere aroma of food could.

"A mess." Veronica shook her head and closed the bathroom door.

Marita had a beautiful vanity in the corner of their private restroom, and Veronica knelt before it.

"Father, forgive me for being anxious and neglecting to have a peaceful night's rest. I know I should've just given the entire situation to You, but I didn't and only hurt me. Father, I need You to help me with my attitude today. I don't want to be grouchy because I'm sleepy. Then, present me with an opportunity to rest in the form of a nap, in Jesus' name. Amen."

Veronica got off her knees and then turned on the shower. When the temperature was just right, she got in and allowed the water from the overhead nozzle to pour on her like rain. Her jet black straight hair became instantly curly. She shampooed and then conditioned her hair. As the conditioner worked to soften her hair, she scrubbed her body with the sweet-smelling lavender soap her grandmother gave her and Selena in their welcome home baskets.

This was her first time visiting her Abuela in years. Although in her mind, she felt like a visitor, in her heart, she'd felt as if they never were separated.

There was something so familiar in abuela's love.

Sort of felt just as the love between her and Valerie did but with a little more freedom. Or was it intensity with gentle ease?

It was indeed different, but there was no mistaking—it was love.

Selena urged her during the ride to just have a one-on-one with Marita to clear the air, but Marita wasn't waiting. As soon as they sat at the table last night, she immediately apologized. For breaking Valerie's heart, letting her oldest daughter walk away with her grandchildren, and for not being the grandmother to her and Vance she should have been.

Although Veronica promised herself she wouldn't cry, that all flew out of the window. They all cried, including Selena, and just as she'd forgiven Selena, she forgave her grandmother.

Veronica dried and lotioned her body with her hair bundled in a fluffy white towel. She laughed when she opened the towel cabinet. Everything was fluffy and white. Now she knew where Her mom had gotten it from...her refusal to buy colored towels. Her mother's towel cabinet was the same as her grandmother's and her spirit of hospitality.

Last night felt like being in the presence of her mother's twin. And by the look of this breakfast spread—yet again—their likeness was absolutely undeniable.

This time, without Selena, she wanted to talk to her grandmother.

"Grandma, do you know English?"

"Girl, who do you think taught your mother and her siblings?"

"Wow, and you speak it nicely."

"Thank you, my sweet Vee."

"I'd like to ask you something."

"Ask away."

"Did you hate black people or just my dad?"

"Honestly, at the time, I just thought Valerie would have a better life if she'd chosen a white husband or her same race. You know, black men have always had it hard in this world. The same people who enslaved them to do work—they were too lazy to accomplish—have the nerve to think all black men are lazy. And at the time, my employer, a white family, hated black people. Do you know how hard my job became? They blamed me for Valerie's choices, and I couldn't afford to quit."

"Wow. Have you ever told my mother this?"

"No. I tried, but to Valerie, there was no excuse to abandon your own child. And in all fairness, she was right. I should have just left the job, but instead, my faith was in that job and those nasty, bigoted people."

"Grandmother, I'm so sorry you had to go through that."

"Baby, they would help to buy food for us and then after that, for three months they only bought us noodles. Then, she cut my hours and wouldn't even pay me my total wages. Wages I worked for."

"I would've have poisoned them."

"No, Veronica. Don't ever say that about anyone. Now you repent, child. Right now."

Veronica mumbled, "Father, forgive me for in my heart, I've murdered a people. In Jesus' name."

"God got them, baby. Everything they did to me came back to them double-fold. She suffered so bad with cancer and, on her death-bed, apologized for everything she did to me. And her husband. He had to raise four teenagers who gave him big troubles. He cried many nights,

53

and he, too, apologized for allowing his wife to handle me the way she did."

"But was that enough for you, Abuela?"

"La venganza es mía, dice el señor. Vengeance is mine saith the Lord, and I remembered this, baby. See, those people who think they're doing something by mistreating you not only reap what they sow, but always reap more than they sowed. And look at my home. All four of those children of theirs make sure I have everything and then some. I will be paid from their parents' estate until the day I die, and even when I'm dead and gone, their money will take care of the upkeep of this home as long as it belongs to our family. See, what the devil meant for bad, God will turn that thing to work for your favor. You better read about Joseph."

"I have. Joseph's own brothers sold him into slavery, and he became their blessed hope in the times of famine."

"You have spoken correctly, my love. And, the very person they hurt had to bless them. That's just how it is with people and my employers. I had to bless both of them, and I watched both of them take their last breath looking at me. I was the last face the Lord allowed either of them to see."

"That's crazy."

"No, baby, that's the Lord. That's why you better be careful who you treat wrong and come up against. And sometimes, white folks feel they are justified in owning slaves, but the Bible told them to remember the slaves they owned belonged to God. They forgot that part. And, to be honest, what we called slaves back then is employees right now. Employers hire you to work to ensure that the master, the CEO, gets great dividends. But you could tell during Covid-19 who truly was doing right by their people and loved God."

"How so?"

"Some businesses that were Christian based were shut all the way down for months. But on the other hand, some mom and pop stores who treated their employees like family survived and also made more money during Covid than they had made in years. See, God was trying to show rich and poor folks something. When you do things His way, you prosper. When you don't, you suffer."

"Abuela, I believe you. Our company never missed a beat, but our owner, Mr. Dwight Esplanada, believes in treating people fairly and correctly. He knows God blessed him to be a blessing, and God multiplied his gain, whereas, some of the companies we are in competition with filed bankruptcy. They went under and quick."

"See, child, God is just and fair and with whatever you give, that you are bound to get in return. Any other way, then our God would be a liar, and He's definitely not that."

Selena came in. "You guys are going deep in here. I was trying to hurry up so I could hear."

"I'm glad you came because there's something I want to say to both of you."

CHAPTER 11

Jessica waited in front of the Law Offices of Jackson/Booth at nine on the dot. She didn't want to be late, and neither did she want to feel anxious, so she did the first and best thing to drinking coffee for comforting oneself: she prayed.

As soon as she said, "Amen," Kane came rushing out of the door.

"Good morning, Mom. How are you?" He leaned in and gave his mother a smack on the cheek.

"Hello, son. All is well."

"So, where are you whisking me off to today? A wedding cake tasting or venue picking?"

"I thought you wanted your wedding on the lawns of our home. There's not a venue in Shreveport that can top mine."

"Don't get testy. Mom, I really don't care where you do it. I just want the woman I love and a preacher, my only two requests."

"Got you, and that's exactly why we are going to see Dr. Day."

"Who is Dr. Day?"

"She's a counselor and, Kane, I want you to have an open mind. I should have taken you to see her when you were six years old, and I saw anger in you I'd never seen before. But you know, I'm guilty of being just like others in my race who feel that all we need is prayer."

"Okay, but, Mom, why didn't you ask me if I wanted to go?"

"Because I knew you'd say no. This is not just about you Kane, it's about me also. As your mother, I always knew I couldn't fill the voids in you, but I ignored that. I tried with everything in me, but I should have been taking you somewhere you could talk about what you were feeling."

"Mom, all you had to do was ask me. Spending money to fix me is ridiculous."

"Kane, you don't need to be fixed. God fixed you when He saved you. Son, this is about enhancing you. Will you just try it and with an opened mind?"

"We're here now," Kane said, glancing at Dr. Day's office. "Let's go get this done."

"Do you still love me?"

"Mom, I will never stop loving you no matter how crazy your ideas get."

Jessica parked the car, turned off the ignition, and said, "Thank you, son."

"Come on girl, so I can get this over with and get back to my office." He waited on his mother to get next to him and then draped his arms around her shoulders.

It brought back so many memories of he and J.J. using her shoulders to measure how tall they'd grown.

Kane opened the door and allowed his mother to go in first. If there were two things Jasper Sr. taught him and J.J., it was to be a gentleman and take care of Jessica and Jasmine.

"Hello, Mr. Jackson Booth and Mrs. Jessica Booth?"

"That's us," Kane answered the receptionist.

"Follow me please," she said, giving them time to walk around her desk. Then leading them down a hallway to a beautiful room that was painted the color of the sea and had all things sea and ocean decorative. "You can sit in here, and I will bring you the drink of your choice."

"No, thank you," Jessica said.

"I'd like a cup of coffee," Kane said.

"Sure. Two or three sugars and cream?"

"Three sugars and three packages of cream would be great."

The receptionist shook her head and said, "I'll be right back."

Kane simply nodded.

"This is such a beautiful and serene room. I feel like I'm in Jamaica looking out on the beautiful aqua-blue ocean."

"Yeah, it's definitely eye-opening, especially with that light from the hinged roof windows. That's neat." Kane tilted his head back.

"It is," Jessica agreed, and they both looked towards the door when they heard it opening.

"Greetings, people of God. I'm Rosalee Day, and it's a pleasure to meet you both."

Kane stood and grabbed Dr. Day's hand in a firm but gentle handshake.

As soon as Kane moved, Jessica and Dr. Day embraced one another with one of those sorority handshakes. Jessica saw something in the display case that solidified Dr. Day as her sister, and a lover of pink, green, and pearls.

After they released one another, Dr. Day took her seat behind the beautiful white desk. No sooner than she sat down, the receptionist knocked twice and entered with Kane's coffee.

Kane reached for the coffee and said, "Thank you."

"You're welcome, Mr. Booth," and she turned and left.

"Before we get started, I'd like to render prayer if that's alright with you both."

"It is," they both answered.

"Great. Father, in the name of the Lord Jesus, we come to you now, Lord, thankful that we are alive. Grateful that You have given us another opportunity of an unwitnessed day. We are thankful, and we still need You. We need You to bless this session. Open the doors to memory and understanding so we can properly place how all things have worked for good. We welcome and love You, in Jesus' name, we pray. Amen."

"Amen," both Jessica and Kane said in unison.

"Jessica, since you are the one who set this meeting up. Tell me, why did the Lord lead you in this direction?"

"Dr. Day, my son has been my son since he was birthed into this world by his mother. At the time, I was trying to get pregnant, but Keisha wasn't. The Lord just blessed her with this sweet baby boy, and because she and I were best friends, she automatically wanted to share Kane Jr. with us. He became ours too. By the time Kane was five, we got pregnant with J.J., and when Kane was nine, we had the baby he named Jasmine."

"So, he's been with you all of his life."

Kane interjected, "Yes, I have, and it's been wonderful."

"Awe, thanks, son. But, Dr. Day, when Jasmine was two, Kane lost both of his parents. They were missionaries who were away on assignment when they died. Well, Kane was with us, but his grandparents—both maternal and paternal—wanted him. Them taking him from us was just as hard as God taking Keisha and Kane Sr. Thanks to God, they had written their desires in a will that had been updated only six months before they left for their trip. It was as though they knew they'd never come back. And they left money for not just Kane, but for all four of us: Jasper, J.J., Jasmine, and myself."

"That's love. So, where does this fit into our today?"

"I don't believe my baby—our baby—got a chance to properly grieve or even share his feelings. When Kane was six, they went away, and he had an angry outburst at school. Jasper Sr. and I went to pick him up, and he expressed that he was angry because his parents left him. We dealt with this situation the best we could, but five years later, they left for good. We tried to give him space to grieve and talked to him, but sometimes I have felt over the years that his in-your-face-attitude is the product of his inability to grieve."

By now, Kane had put his coffee on the table. He looked as if he'd taken another sip, he would have regurgitated.

"Kane, I see something was said that affected you. Why don't you tell me what you're thinking."

Tears immediately began to flow from Kane's eyes.

"We'll give you a moment," and Dr. Day prayed. "Father, help Him put what he's feeling into words, in Jesus' name."

"Mom, first, I'm so grateful to have you and Dad. I'm also even more thankful you all made me a Booth at my request. Sometimes, I wonder what life would've been like with them, Keisha and Kane, but I'm old enough to know that God makes no mistakes."

"I felt that, Kane," Dr. Day interjected.

"Thanks, I guess. I just know that I have lashed out at people but I believe that if I don't say what I feel, the moment might come, and I can't."

"Because, you were not allowed to say what you felt about your parents leaving you, huh?"

"Yes. Like, who has a child and then keeps leaving them to go win others' souls? Aren't you neglecting the soul God gave you to nurture?"

"Kane, so you heard that Keisha wasn't trying to get pregnant but, Jessica was. Do you blame Jessica for always readily accepting the task of keeping you? Should she have made them take their own baby with them?"

"No, Ma'am, I could never blame my Momma. I'm so thankful she wanted me. But, I can blame them for leaving me. I just sometimes always go back to why God would allow them to be so concerned with others but not me."

"No, Kane, they were concerned," Jessica interjected. "They made sure you had everything you needed, and us to care for you in their absence."

"This is how I see it. Kane, your parents, were called by God for an assignment greater than them. One assignment was to win souls, but the other was to give Jasper and Jessica a baby boy named, Kane Jackson-Booth. God works in mysterious ways, and although we can't always trace His ways, we can track them. And if we track your situation, we see unselfishness, love, devotion, commitment, a calling, and a sacrifice."

"Wow, I never thought of it like that."

"Me either," Jessica chimed in.

"God makes no mistakes. He's sovereign. God is God. He can do whatever He wants to do. Sometimes it's not always favorable to us—at least it seems—but the reality is, His favor is not always fair. So what if they had taken you?"

"I'd be dead too."

"Okay, so was the trade necessary or fair?"

"What do you mean by trade?" Kane asked.

"They traded time with their son, for their son having time on earth. Now, you tell me, was it necessary?"

"By all means, it was, because I'd much rather be alive and exploring if I'd ever be as committed to God as they were."

"And they were committed. Much more than I'd ever been," Jessica said.

"Sometimes, this race gets hard, Kane. And sometimes, you make decisions that are absolutely connected to your destiny. In your moments of anger, did you ever think your parents made the wrong decision? Was leaving you with the Booths instead of your grandparents wrong?"

"Heaven no. I'm so glad they took care of my parents' situation. Oh, my God, I'm so grateful for you all, mom," Kane wrapped his arms around Jessica's neck. She was now crying so hard that Dr. Day had to come from behind the desk to console her.

"Sis, you got this. God did not allow you to bring yourself nor your son here so that the answers to the hard things won't be unveiled. It's the unveiling of these things that ushers us into complete healing and spiritual wholeness. You do want Kane whole don't you?"

Jessica, through sniffles, nodded her head.

"Well, God is going to meet you both today at a point of understanding that will shock you into tears, but at the same time into wholeness. I'm not telling you not to cry, my sister. But I'm just suggesting that while you cry, you add a few thank you Jesus' to the tears. I promise he has you, and because you're my sister—the one who bleeds the same blood as me. The one who I know will never leave me in the trenches alone. The one who has made an oath to cover me with your heart, help me with your hands, pray for me with your mouth, and bless me with your substances...must understand that I have you now. This session has become one hundred times deeper to me because we're family."

"I love you, my sister," Jessica said. She squeezed Dr. Day even tighter. All over the world, God had allowed women who could only recognize one another through a symbol, colors, or their love, become how He wanted all of His daughters to be towards one another. And this display of love alone gave Jessica all the strength she needed to dry her tears and be right there with the son God gave her.

"You good now?" Dr. Day asked Jessica.

"All is well," Jessica smiled.

"Okay, Kane, are you okay?" Dr. Day turned her focus back to Kane.

"I am, and my heart is racing to see my mother interact with someone who showed her the love she shows others."

"All I can say is that's what we do." Dr. Day winked at Kane, and he started laughing.

"See, when I think of you, Kane, I'm reminded of Moses. He was born to Jochebed and Amram, two from the tribe of Levi, who lived in Egypt when the children of Israel lived as slaves. Moses was the youngest of three children and had a sister named Miriam and a brother named Aaron. The Pharaoh was afraid of the Israelite slaves because they were multiplying, so he ordered that the baby boys be killed. His mother, Jochebed, hid him three months to save his life. When she could no longer hide him, she waterproofed a basket and put him in the Nile River. When the daughter of Pharaoh went to bathe in the Nile, she spotted the baskets wrapped in reeds and sent her maidservants to get it. Well, to her surprise, in the basket was a baby boy. She knew he was a Hebrew baby, but she had compassion on him. Moses' sister, who was an attendant, set the stage for her mother to be brought in to nurse the baby. His very own mother was paid to nurse him until he was older, and when she weaned the baby, she took the baby back to Pharaoh's daughter, who named him Moses and raised him in the palace surrounded by all the luxuries of Egypt."

CHAPTER 12

Selena pulled out a chair next to Veronica and hurriedly scooted up close to the table so she could hear what Abuela wanted to tell her two granddaughters.

"Go ahead and fix your plate, Selena. You both can eat while I talk."

"Yes, Ma'am," Selena reached for two torrijas and scooped some chilaquiles mixed with eggs, steak, and shredded cheese onto her plate. "What?" Selena asked as she looked at Veronica.

"Nothing, greedy. Just hurry so Abuela can tell us what she has to say."

"I'm hurrying." Selena poured her a cup of hot coffee and then said, "Now."

Marita began to speak, "Estoy muy orgullosa de ustedes chicas," then she shook her head and repeated in English what she said. "I'm so proud of you girls because you brought this family together, in ways I'd only prayed years for. Tu papa esta sonriendo desde el cielo (Your dad is smiling down from heaven). One day he drove by my house and stopped when he saw me standing outside. I apologized to him for my stupidity. I always wanted what's best for all of my children, and he was what was best for you all. After he passed, I reached out to Valerie, but she thought I wanted money, too, since her brother Pablo had already called

—begging. Your dad told me that even if he's in heaven, you, Veronica, and you, Selena, would be the best of friends, and he'd be in heaven smiling. And, chicas, I believe him. I believe he's smiling down on you two right now."

Both Veronica and Selena no longer held their forks but instead—one another's hand—as tears streamed down both of their faces.

"Bien, no se separen," Marita wrapped her arms around both of them.

"We will not separate, Abuela," they both said in unison.

"If there's one thing I know, todas las niñas buenas van al cielo (all good girls go to heaven). My prayer has always been, Espíritu de vida y amor, renuévanos en la unidad. Amen. (Spirit of life and of love, renew us in unity. Amen.) And God is answering my prayers."

Selena smiled. "Dios seguro es abuela (God sure is grandmother)."

Veronica said, "Amén."

"Now, chicas, hurry up and finish your food. You girls have a long day ahead of you, and your nonna has to go to the market."

"Do I need to drive you?" Selena asked.

"No, take care of the business before you, and Cecilia will take me as usual."

"Perfect. We'll see you when you get back or if you beat us back, when we get back."

***

CRAWL WATCHED as Selena's Abuela got in the car with her friend. There were still no signs of she and Veronica, but he knew eventually they'd come out, and he'd be right behind them. He was more than happy Chief Linnear put him on the assignment, but he was also leery.

Not because he had doubts about the job.

But he never wanted to put Selena in any danger. And if Rufus' crew saw him with her, it would knock his street creds clean out. Right now, everyone thought he was in hiding because he'd killed D2. At least, that was the word on the streets.

If only they knew.

His only aspiration was to make sure he took care of this amazing woman and her family. And if his calculations were correct, he'd have this assignment done and behind him by mid-July.

He looked up just in time to see Selena coming out of the house. She wore a beautiful teal-colored knee-length sundress, and the white sandals made it easy to see her toenails were the color of her dress. The elderly neighbor was shouting something that must've acknowledged her outfit because Selena smiled and twirled around like a little girl showing off her dress.

Damon's heart melted.

That she would oblige the elderly showed just how beautiful her heart was.

She looked across in his direction and flashed what he thought was a smile. He shook his head because he couldn't believe the face that was startled in shock at the sight of him was now pleasingly smiling. Now, all he had to do was wait at the right moment to approach her.

A few minutes later, her cousin, Veronica, emerged from the house. She wore a beautiful soft yellow pantsuit perfectly fit for spring. She waved at the neighbors and quickly made her way to the passenger side of the car.

He mumbled, "Hurry up and get in your car, Selena." The less she stood outside the car, the more protected she'd be.

Finally, she got in, and as she started her engine, he started his. He waited a few minutes to leave after her because the less suspicious the neighbors were, the better for him. Chief had a tracker put on the car she'd drive while in town, so he wasn't afraid of losing her.

She was supposed to be going to the home she shared with Rufus, Rufus' mother's home, and then back to her house. He tapped the button on his car to play Calvin Richardson's Gold Dust album. He flipped to "She Never Had A Real Man Like This," because she hadn't, but sooner or later, she'd have him…a real man.

Tomorrow, she'd sit at the funeral of Rufus. Someone who vowed to love her but loved himself more. Damon grooved to the music as he caught up to them. He pulled into the neighbor's driveway and watched as she and Veronica entered the house.

༺꠶༻

"VEE, he's parking in the neighbor's driveway. I hope he made sure no one was in this house."

"They probably have cameras all over this house, since Rufus ties to the street were so elaborate. Let's go in and get what you came here for, so we can leave quickly."

"I feel you. This house has so many bad memories until I don't want to be here a minute longer than I have to be."

They pulled outside of the garage, but Selena opened it. She had to make sure no one was there. Selena unlocked the door, and she and Veronica went in. The house was spotless, and she was thankful their housekeeper was still working.

Selena walked into her room. All her boxes were packed and sitting in the middle of the floor. She was even more grateful than she was at first. Not only had Rema cleaned the house, but she'd also packed all of her belongings.

"That housekeeper is the bomb. I wish I could pack her up and bring her to Louisiana with us."

"She's phenomenal, but you know what?"

"What, Selena?"

"Instead of selling this house, I think I'd give it to Rema. She and her children could use this four-bedroom home. She's staying in a two-bedroom with six children and a husband. This way, the children could share rooms, and she and hubby will have a room."

"Cousin, that's so sweet. I'm sure she'd love it. But would she be able to pay the bills?"

"I'll pay them up for a year, and then she can use the money she makes to save. I'll continue to pay the taxes and do Rema like Abuela's employer's family did her."

"Like paying it forward."

"Exactly."

"Cousin, I think it's a wonderful idea. I know I'd be happy and praising the Lord if you did that for my family and me."

"Well, that's that. Let me get my sketches and music."

"Sketches and music?"

"I wasn't just a shopping housewife, Vee. I've been writing music for some of the local artists for years. I've also found so much peace when I'm drawing. See..." Selena unrolled a picture and showed it to Veronica.

"Selena, that's beautiful. That's Abuela, auntie Vashti, and my mom!"

"I know, silly. It's how I've always wanted them to be. Together."

"They will, and I promise we'll make it happen. You should have seen my mom when aunt Vashti and uncle Aaron came to her reception dinner. She was so happy. Now, we just have to get all three of them together."

"It's time. We are family, and it's time we act like it."

"Amen."

CHAPTER 13

K ane listened attentively as Dr. Day told the story about Moses. Jasper and Jessica didn't have to get him out of the water, but they did rescue him. There was no way he would be able to have the life he's had with his grandparents. And for the first time in his life, he was more than confident his parents did what they had to do to keep him alive and give him the life they always wanted for him.

And to think he never felt a single ounce of difference between he and J.J. was a testament of their love. The same way Jessica or Jasper would fight for their biological children, they fought for him. He never felt jealousy or envy in their home, and when he and J.J. had their one and only fight, they both got a whipping.

A good one.

One that made them rethink hard about ever putting a hand on one another.

Although his name didn't start with a J, it ended with Booth, which was more than enough for him. Dad had even adapted to calling them K.J. and J.J. when they were young and sometimes even now.

"Do you see the provisions made for you, Mr. Booth?"

"I surely do. My parents left nothing to chance, and with the help of the Lord, they secured the greatest future for their son. I'm honored, appreciative, and now I realize just how blessed I am."

"Now, what triggered this meeting? Why did your mother think it so important to get you in here to me?"

"Because I got angry and hung up the phone on my fiancée. She made the suggestion to separate for a minute, and I blew up."

"Could that be directly linked to your feelings of abandonment?"

"At first, I would have never associated it with that...but now I see it. Her even suggesting to leave me cut me in a scar that I never knew was there. It hurt that she would even suggest us splitting up just to keep us from sex."

"Jessica, could you give us a few? Just wait out in the receptionist area, and if you'd like anything to eat or snack on, tell Christy to get what you need."

"Yes, that would be great." Jessica stood and kissed Kane on the head. "Thanks, Mom."

"I'll see you when you finish," Jessica said as she was leaving the room.

"Okay, I know it's uncomfortable talking about certain things with Mom in the room. So, have you both agreed on waiting until marriage before sex?"

"Yes, we made a commitment to stay celibate until we stood before a preacher. These feelings just started coming at me like crazy."

"Son, that's normal. I say to my members that if men didn't initiate sex, some women wouldn't have it. But making a vow to God and keeping it means everything. He even said in His Word, that it would be better not to make a vow than to make one and turn from it. It means a lot to God when you promise Him something but do something else. He knows the pressures you have staying pure from fornication. He also knows the pressures men have versus women. But real men make sure everything is decent and in order before they go there. Look at Boaz, he made sure that the kinsman-redeemer had no desire to take Ruth, Mahlon's widow, as his wife, but as soon as the sandal was removed and given to Boaz, he took Ruth home, and she became his wife. And the

Bible says, when he had relations with her, the Lord enabled her to conceive, and she gave birth to a son.'"

"Okay, so what are you saying?"

"I believe that what you have with Veronica is blessed by the Lord. I hear the Lord saying, 'the moment you lay with her, she becomes your wife' and He will enable her to conceive. I do not speak it if I do not hear Him say it. For your seed to be blessed, God allowed this blowup to keep you both from making the wrong decision."

"Wow."

"Yes, God has a way. She is definitely your wife, and you will bear fruit with her and be blessed all of your lives."

"I receive that in Jesus' name."

"Sometimes, Kane, we have to look at the whole picture instead of pieces. And when the pieces start to upset us, it's time to back away and pray."

"She did leave, and Mom forbade me to go behind her. Now, I'm glad she did."

"All things really do work together for our good. We just have to believe that. Now, how are you planning to make things right with Veronica?"

"I'm going to pray about it, but I promise I'm going to explain why I did what I did as soon as possible."

"Maybe you should wait until she gets home. Maybe, this is the perfect moment for you to show her and tell her exactly what you feel."

"Thank you, Dr. Day. I appreciate you for moving your schedule around to accommodate us."

"You are welcome. Now, if you ever need to talk again, I'm here. But I'm godly-certain, that all you'll need is a good Word on Sunday morning to keep you in perfect alignment."

"Awesome. Thanks again." Kane stood and extended his hand towards Dr. Day.

She shook his hand. "I'll be waiting for my invite."

"For sure," Kane said as he walked out of the door and then realized Dr. Day was coming behind him.

"I'm just going to say goodbye to your mother. I definitely appreciate her for even thinking I could help her baby."

"Hey there," Jessica said when she saw Kane come through the door.

"Hey, Mom, I'm done," Kane said, pulling his mother up from the seat she sat comfortably in.

"Mrs. Booth, thank you for trusting God in me." Dr. Day stretched out her hand towards Jessica.

"No, Ma'am, I'm a hugger. We are covered by the blood of Jesus, so I can greet you with a hug, my sister."

"Jessica, I feel the exact same." They hugged one another. "Now, just because we are covered doesn't make us free to go hug crazy."

"Amen, Day. Trust me. I'm hugging in moderation. I've lost some people who were dear to my heart behind that disease, but I also had to encourage myself because God only takes those who are ready to go."

"Yes, my sister. I can't imagine going to heaven and then turning back around and coming back here because of those I've left behind. I just believe that nothing will be able to compare to me seeing Jesus face to face."

"I hear you, and I feel the same. I love my family, but I have just as many family members in heaven too. I just believe that He only takes those who have decided that they are ready to be with Him. God is so good, Day."

"Who are you telling? This girl is just like Kane's parents...I've given my entire life to Him, and sometimes it interferes with relationships on earth, but I'm alright with that. I chose to live and die for Him, and all the in-betweens He will work them out in my best interest."

"Yes. Well, thank you again, and I promise just to see my baby smiling like he's smiling right now, that's worth more than the money I've spent for this session. God knows who will be a blessing to our children."

"Amen. And I'm so grateful to be used by Him. I'll be seeing you around FTC sometime soon. Your pastor has been a jewel."

"That he is. First Lady Destiny, too. I love that entire family."

"So do I."

"Well, let me get out here so I can get my baby back to his office. We've made perfect timing, so I guess I'll treat him to lunch."

"You all enjoy and be blessed."

"Same to you, Dr. Day. Goodbye, Christy."

"Bye Mrs. Booth. Nice meeting you."

"You too. And you both have a wonderful day."

"We will," both Dr. Day and Christy said at the same time.

CHAPTER 14

Damon could hardly believe his eyes. Two of their officers were circling around the block and watching Rufus' house. He immediately got down low so they wouldn't see him in the car and called Chief Linnear.

"Chief, I'm outside of Burns home waiting on Selena and Veronica to come out, and I notice Officers Rainey and Clutchens blocking. Both are in squad cars, but they look like they're in plain clothes. Looks like we got the last two ducks. Okay, so call them and tell them not to come out."

"Done." Chief hung up from Damon and dialed Selena's phone.

"Hello, Chief," she answered on the second ring.

"Look, I want you and Veronica to stay inside. Stay away from the windows and do not open the door. Both Damon and myself have keys, and we are the only two people besides the cleaning lady who can get in."

"Okay, but how did they know I was here."

"That's what I'm trying to figure out. Just stay down, and I will have answers soon."

Selena grabbed Veronica by the hand and pulled her down to the floor. She motioned for Veronica to follow her, and they crawled to the room that was Rufus' man's cave. Once they got there, Selena moved a rug and opened a hidden door in the floor. When they were safely in the secret room, Selena turned on lights and the televisions on the wall. Every screen showed them exactly what was going on at every angle. And just as Chief said, two cars kept riding by, and Selena snapped pictures of both vehicles and had a clear vision of each man.

There was an angle from the light pole which she was able to get pictures of the assault weapons they had on their seats.

She immediately sent a picture to Chief Linnear, and he called her phone.

"I'm not going to ask how you got those pictures, but Damon is behind the hedges on the side of your home if they get out, and we have some undercover cars en route."

"Okay," Selena said as she flipped the camera on the left side to see Damon. "Darn, he's cute."

"He sure is," Veronica agreed.

"And he's willing to get out his car to protect you. I say he just may be the one, cousin."

"Come on, Veronica, let's pray. Father, please help us. Don't let these evil men do anything to Damon or us. Protect us, Jesus, and please let the men chief sent hurry."

"In Jesus' name," Veronica said.

When both Rainey and Clutchens thought it was safe for them to park, they both parked, and Selena could see them putting on masks.

"Vee, they really want me dead."

"Girl, the devil in them is a lie. I will not lose you."

The crooked cops knocked on the door as if she would actually allow them to come in. She could see them tampering with the lock, but what they didn't know was Rufus wasn't crazy. Every door appeared to have only one deadbolt from the outside, but inside, there were three more locks.

Selena would never forget the first time she visited this home. Her mind drifted back...

"Why do you have these locks? Who are you afraid of?"

Rufus looked at her, puzzled, then spoke, "Girl, you must not understand

78

how many criminals I arrest. One thing is for sure, I'll be protected in my own home if nowhere else."

Selena didn't realize how wide his protection expanded—at that point—but she later found out.

"No one can get in this house, Vee. And if Rufus didn't want you out of it, you couldn't get out either. One day I got mad at him, and he held me, hostage, in this house for more than two weeks. I couldn't get out for nothing. So, they'll be picking at that lock forever, because every lock and window is criminal-proofed."

"Look at them. They're really exhorting energy trying to get to you."

"Yep, and it's taking the cops forever," Selena said and then pointed at the screen.

Undercover cops were coming from all kinds of directions. Rainey and Clutchens were on the ground, and they watched Damon quickly get back in his blacked-out car next door. He was watching everything, just like they were.

Selena asked Veronica to move quick as Chief Linnear read the two cops their Miranda rights. They rushed around, turned off the screens and lights, climbed out of the secret room, closed the door, pulled the rug back over the door, and sat on the floor with their backs against the sofa as if they'd been there. Selena told Vee she didn't want anyone to know about the room she'd discovered months ago. She wanted to explore it first and then she'd tell someone about it.

This is why she was having second thoughts about giving the home to Rema. Maybe she'd just buy her one but allow her to pick it and keep this home for whenever she was in town. And at that point, she made up her mind to stay in her own home tonight.

Once all the units were gone, both Chief Linnear and Damon came inside.

Chief Linnear grabbed both Selena and Veronica by the hand, "Are you, ladies, alright?"

"Yes, sir," they both answered.

"Well, looks like the streets of Dade County are better. I keep telling my staff once all the bad cops are locked up, all the good cops can show people what real policing is about. Serving and protecting."

"Amen, because I really feel bad for all the cops who get a bad rep for the few that are bad," Selena said.

"And it never fails. It's always the good cops like my dad who get killed. It's never the racist, mean-spirited ones who die. But then again, that's another look at God's grace. He is simply taking those who are ready and giving those who aren't more time to get ready," Veronica added.

Damon shook his head. "But to think how some never get ready... baffles me."

Chief Linnear patted him on the shoulder. "Now we know what Paul meant when he asked the question, 'how much longer will grace abound?' Sometimes, they think they are already living in hell. Thus causing them not to anticipate the hell that's prepared for those who fail to believe. But, hey, I guess since no one has technically gone there and came back to tell them the truth, they still think it's false. But as for me and my house and my department, we will serve the Lord. And we will be the kind of law-abiding officers that the city can be proud of."

"Wonderful." Veronica hugged Chief Linnear, "I know my dad would still be proud to call you brother and friend."

Now, Chief Linnear's eyes were watering up. No one knew how committed he was to getting Rufus and the rest of the crooked cops off the street but his wife and his pal the late Vance Kimbrel, Sr.

"This one's for you, friend." Chief Linnear pointed towards heaven.

"Now, are you ladies going back to Marita's house?" Chief asked, causing both Selena and Vee to look at one another.

"I guess we can stay here tonight, but we do have to go back to Marita's to get our clothes," Selena answered.

"Well, I still want Damon to stick around if it's okay with you, ladies. Maybe, he can stay here with you all. Damon, I'd also feel better if you drive them to Marita's. I feel like we finally have all of Rufus' gang in jail now, but you never know. So, until these ladies leave for Louisiana, I want you with them at all times."

"Roger that, Chief."

"Okay, so I'm going to get back home to wifey. I will see you both at the memorial tomorrow." Both Selena and Veronica nodded. "Alright, our little, Vee. No matter how grown you get, you'll always be our little Vee."

"I accept that." Veronica smiled, hugged him, and gave him a kiss on the cheek.

"Damon, come on, walk me out, and we'll let you girls get your purses out of the car. Don't open the garage and leave out of this door. I still have surveillance around and I will continue to have it that way until you both are back at home."

"Okay," the both answered.

Damon walked behind Chief asking, "Who was the leak?"

"Marita told Lucy who is Clutchens' Abuela. Small world."

"Chief, too small if you asked me," Damon replied.

CHAPTER 15

Jessica made her famous meatloaf with mashed potatoes, green beans, and fresh homemade rolls. She even made a chocolate cake to sweeten the deal because when it came to her children if she mentioned food, they were all in.

And tonight, she needed full and complete cooperation.

Kane was the first to arrive.

He looked refreshed, but his eyes, which were the windows to his soul, looked burdened. Jessica already knew the boy was in his head about Veronica, but after tonight, he would be on a mission.

Kane was over an hour early, and this was more than alright with Jessica. She told him to wash his hands and watch her food until she was dressed. Even for dinner at home, Jessica always made sure she looked like the queen of the family.

Ten minutes after she made her way back to the kitchen, J.J., Jade, Valerie, James, Jasmine, and Vance all pulled up at the same time. Kane opened the door for their family and escorted everyone to the family room where Jasper sat watching the latest episode of The Voice.

He muted the television as his family came in because of his strict directives. He offered his brother and sons a drink, but no one wanted one. By the time he'd sat on the piano bench, Jessica came in greeting everyone with a hug and kiss.

"Family, I know you all are wondering why I called you over, so let me get to it. Kane did something so crazy, and he fully regrets it...even though he knows it's going to take a strong prayer and notion to win Veronica back. Am I right, Kane?"

Kane shook his head. "Yes, Mother, you are right."

"Dad, why didn't you teach this boy something? He's a mess." J.J. laughed.

"J.J., I taught him the same thing I taught you and look at how your situation turned out." Jasper put both his hands up, looking like the inquisitive emoji.

"I bet you'll stop picking now," Uncle James told J.J., and everyone laughed.

"Has anyone even heard from Veronica?" Jessica asked.

Everyone in the room pretty much answered no except Valerie.

"Well, she did call me, but she wouldn't discuss anything about her and Kane. I stopped pushing when I realized she was getting upset. But if I know my daughter, she's thrown herself into helping Selena so she can forget all about her own pain."

"I understand, Valerie. So, this is why I've called the family together. Kane did something crazy, but he loves Veronica, and we all want them to be happy. So, I was thinking...why don't we plan the wedding, and as soon as she gets off that airplane, let's move into action. She'll think we are taking her to a surprise place to have dinner with an apologetic Kane, but we'll hide all the cars by the boat ramp on the west side of the house and set up a beautiful gazebo on the east side. The only person she will see is Kane until he asks her to marry him again. When and if she says, 'yes,' the preacher and all of us will come out from all directions. And it will be the surprise wedding of a lifetime. We will have enormous tents in the back she will not be able to see for the wall."

"So, the wedding will be on the front side, and once she gets past the wall, she'll see all the fanfare of an outdoor wedding," Jasmine said.

"Exactly." Jessica nodded and smiled. Because little did Jasmine

84

know, she'd be dressed for what Jessica envisioned to be the best double surprise wedding either of them had ever seen.

"Aw, Mom, that's going to be wonderful." Jasmine got up from where she was seated and hugged her mom.

"I'm in, Momma J," Jade added. "Now, when will we start the planning."

"I've already started it, and I want you and Jasmine to be dressed as brides. A glamorized Cinderella moment with all three of my girls." Jessica clapped her hands together.

"Mom, you are so silly. You're going to have all of us looking really crazy." Jasmine laughed.

"No, you will be beautiful, and Veronica always wanted her brides-maids to be dressed as princesses. And will all of us wear formal as well?" Valerie asked.

"Sis, you do know me. Yes. We will all be decked out in our formal-wear, and this event will be even more beautiful than the Christmas in the Field." Jessica smiled as she looked at the faces of her family. Everyone was all in, and only three people knew her secret...Kane, Vance, and Valerie. She could have never pulled it off by herself, but even Jasper Sr. would be surprised that he'd get a chance to walk his baby down the aisles. Jasmine will think her dad is just escorting her in since Vance is the best man, and then she'll realize he's a groomsman.

That's all Jasper had ever wanted, but with the situation as it was, he couldn't be upset that Jasmine and Vance had chosen to marry on Valen-tine's Day in the hospital. Given she could have lost him, Jasper would have been a fool to interrupt their plans. That still didn't stop him from secretly hurting.

And now, Jessica had the perfect opportunity to do what every wife should inspire to do...take away her husband's pain.

"So, everyone's in?" Jessica asked her family, who was conversing about how awesome the surprise would be.

"Yes," they all answered together.

Jessica threw up her hands. "Hallelujah! This will be perfect. Now, if you all would go and wash your hands and meet me in the kitchen, Jasper can pray, and we can eat."

"All you have to do is tell me once," J.J. said as he tried to beat Kane to the restroom. They were running like little boys, and it did Jessica's heart all the good to see her men being boys.

Jessica put the food on the table, and everyone claimed their seat. Once she was in her chair, Jasper asked the family to bow their heads for prayer. He blessed the food, and the conversations began.

"Jasmine, how's married life treating you and Vance?"

"Dad, he's been the perfect gentleman," Jasmine answered her dad but touched Vance on his shoulder.

"And she's so much like Mrs. Jessica until it's crazy. I can't believe she's the same woman y'all talked about shopping and spending tons of money. I don't know what happened, but this woman is constantly talking about saving money," Vance caused everyone—except Valerie's— eyes to furrow.

They all only knew the Jasmine who would *shop until you dropped.*

"My brother, you are a king amongst kings, because anyone who can make my baby sister choose saving over Prada and Gucci has got to be a real man," J.J. said, and Kane agreed.

Jasmine's brow wrinkled. "Really, brothers. So, you're gonna put all my junk in the atmosphere like that."

J.J. laughed, but Kane stated, "It's the truth."

"My old truth, but now I understand the importance of making me rich instead of all those designers. Vance made me see how being a good steward over your finances also meant embracing the power to get wealth, which sometimes came by saving instead of spending."

"Amen. I'm glad someone got through to you. Jasper, had I known Vance was all it took, I would have paid him to marry her when we gave her that trust fund."

"Mom! I know you didn't go there. Not the woman who always told me to spend big or not at all. You are the reason I know clothes and shoes. If you would have bought me stuff from Wally World instead of Dillards, maybe I'd buy cheap."

"Uh-hum, she's got a point there." Jasper, Sr. nodded.

"You just stay at the head of this table and eat your food. No one asked for your opinion, Mr. Booth." Jessica hit Jasper with her napkin.

"Don't be hitting my daddy for telling his truth. You know you're the cause of all of our tastes. And then you told us if a man didn't wear good shoes, he couldn't take care of a woman," Kane retorted.

"Her exact words, 'How can you take care of a woman and you won't even take care of your own feet. Can't no man take care of me who won't cherish what he needs to keep him working,'" J.J., Kane, and Jasper said it together causing everyone to burst into laughter. Especially, how Kane was working his neck and J.J. was doing his hands.

"And don't forget this, 'If a Booth-man don't work, he won't eat or sleep, especially up in anything I call mine,'" J.J. added.

"Case in point. Our children—all three of them—are exactly like the woman who nurtured them." Jasper leaned in and kissed Jessica.

CHAPTER 16

Selena and Veronica rode in silence to Marita's house. Had Damon not been driving them, they would have been talking about him. Veronica slid her hand between the front seat and the door to hit Selena, who tilted her head a little.

Veronica pinched her.

"Crawl," Selena responded to the pinch.

"Yes, Selena."

"How long have you been an undercover cop?"

"I joined the force when I turned twenty-one. My dad told me that since the street knew me as Crawl, I should just be undercover."

"Okay, so you knew about Rufus all along?"

"Yes, I actually got close to him to protect you."

"I knew it!"

"No, you didn't." Damon laughed and poked Selena on the side.

"I did too. I even told Veronica that sometimes you would look at me so strange. If I didn't know any better, I would have sworn you were trying to hit on me."

"Maybe I was doing a little too much."

"So, you were trying to get me to notice you?"

"Not exactly. I wanted you to feel safe around me and not have the look of fear in your eyes. Especially like the one you had the day you brought this case to a head."

"You have to understand by then God was talking to me. Telling me to get away from Rufus, and when I opened the garage and saw you there, I almost freaked out."

"I saw. But to think, I was getting ready to blow my cover to you."

"You were going to do what?"

"Selena, my feelings were changing for you. I'd saw him hit you before. I wanted to kill that dude. So, I started coming around more to make sure he didn't put his hands on you. And the night before, I'd had enough. I was coming to tell you to hide out at my house, but you had to leave that monster."

"You felt he was a monster?"

"I'd seen him do some horrible things, Selena. Hurt a lot of people."

"So, you wanted to protect me?"

"Yes."

"Protecting you is why Chief gave me the job. He needed someone who knew the streets, and the police knew was hard. That way, if Rufus was beating you, I would get him off of you. Even if…"

"What?"

"Even if I had to hurt him. Like the day he hit you, and I threw him off you. He was mad at me, but I didn't care. I would have popped him that day and claimed self-defense as the motive. First, he hit you, and then he hit you like you were a man. You didn't deserve any of that."

By now, Selena was crying, and Veronica was sitting up rubbing her cousin's shoulders.

Selena whispered, "God didn't just start protecting me?"

"I told you that," Veronica chimed in. "Thank you, Crawl, Damon—or whatever name you prefer to go by—for staying around for Selena."

"Veronica, you don't have to thank me. It was all my pleasure, and Selena is a good woman. She cooked, made sure the housekeeper was on point, and tried to make sure her husband happy. He was just too dumb to see what was standing before him. As a matter of fact, Veronica, he was too in love with you."

Veronica's eyebrows squinted. "How do you know that?"

"Rufus told me. He was bold in his confession but was also pissed when you chose Kane over him."

"You know, Kane?"

"Rufus told me everything about him. He even knew that Kane was the better man for you, but he couldn't hardly stand the rejection from you. Then again, when we lose the women we really love, we spend a lifetime trying to find her in other women or treating women like we would never think of treating the woman we loved."

"Wow."

"And to think I actually thought that he'd eventually come to love me. I knew he loved you, Veronica. I just thought since you were gone, he'd look at me how he used to look at you," Selena said through sniffles.

Damon interrupted, "Oh, so you wanted Rufus to look at you like I look at you? He wasn't capable, Selena, but I am. I will always look at you just how you need to be admired."

"Huh?" Selena acted as though she needed him to repeat himself.

"You heard me." Damon stroked a finger against her cheek. "No man will ever look at you like I'll look at you. I see you, Selena. I've seen you since the first day you walked into Coral Reef High School with those peach sandals that complemented that peach and turquoise sundress. I saw you then, and Selena, I see you now."

"Wow. You remember that dress?"

"How could I forget it, or you?"

"You never acted as if you were interested."

"Okay, let's go back. It was three days before our senior prom, and I'd heard you were going alone. I came to your locker, and you were standing with Diego talking about your uncle's death. When you started to cry, I gave you some tissue and you thanked me, but you probably thought that nut cared enough to provide you with tissues to wipe your tears. Do you remember?"

"That was you? My eyes were so wet, I thought Diego gave them to me. And then he grabbed me as if he did."

"To keep you away from me. But like I told him then, and I'm telling you now, you cannot take from a man what God used him to create.

Selena, even if you reject me now one day, you'll be in my arms and stay right there until the day God takes His breath from you."

Selena's breath was caught, and she couldn't say anything.

"You don't have to say anything because I don't need a response to what's factual. When God created me in the heavens, He took you from my rib and placed you in your daddy's loins, and you know how the rest goes. The reality is, we were constructed by God, connected in heaven, and considered because of His grace. Now all you have to do is consider the favor that He has placed over our lives and then determine that favor ain't fair."

"Damon, that's deep," Veronica said when she realized her cousin was too shocked to say anything. Selena just sat there staring at Damon as if she were looking at the ghost of love.

By the time Damon pulled in Marita's parking space, Selena's face was stained with tears. Damon did precisely what he should have done that day in school.

He wiped her tears.

And Selena did what she actually should have done years ago —let him.

❧

VERONICA WATCHED the events unfolding in front of her as if she was watching a love story written by one of the best romance authors.

The words were leaping out of Damon's mouth but hitting her heart. She knew what she had to do.

Veronica had to make things better with Kane.

She understood why she'd reacted to his assumption as she did. For her, it felt like rejection. The same kind she'd gotten from Rufus. But in truth, he only got that mad because he probably thought that he was being rejected by her.

Watching firsthand what was going on between Selena and Damon, Veronica realized love was so worth having. *And the shame of you finally realizing it was there all along, but you just looked over it or allowed it to pass you by, was a pitiful shame.*

She wasn't having it. Love was not passing her by.

Veronica's mind shifted. *Selena could have been sheltered from all the hurt and pain she'd experienced, but like most women, she didn't see the love that was staring her right in the face.*

"Veronica. Veronica."

Veronica shook her head as if to shake back into her now. "You called me?"

"We're here, and we need to get our stuff and hurry."

"No, cousin. I'm staying at abuela's house, and you and Damon should go. I love you, and I'm so happy for you."

CHAPTER 17

J asmine pulled her car into their garage and then turned to face Vance. She was so grateful that God spared his life but even more grateful to wear Kimbrel as her last name.

"Baby, do you think Mom can pull this wedding off?"

"Girl, we are talking about your mother. Momma J is the second strongest woman I know, and you know when she wants something done, it happens."

"Listening to her plan, Kane and Veronica's wedding, I almost regret not allowing her to give me a wedding."

"Just the wedding and not marrying me, right?"

"Babe, I could never regret marrying you. I would have married you in a shoebox—next to a toilet—just to be with you. You have been the perfect husband, and now I just want to become the best wife I can be."

"You're already that. So, spend your time creating a goal like becoming the best mother you can be."

"Are you sure you're ready for children? They're a huge responsibility."

"I'm not threatened by that, Jas. With us as their parents, they are going to be a great asset to society and Christianity."

"Okay, I hear you, Daddy."

"You better. Now, all that wedding talk is making me want to celebrate our marriage. How quick can you meet me in your favorite position?"

"As quick as you can, put us on some music and pour us two glasses of wine."

"I'm on it."

"And I'm going to kiss you to make sure you have the anointing to move quick."

Vance laughed, "Girl, I don't need the anointing to move quick. I just need to know you gonna show me what you're working with."

"I got you, boo. See you in five minutes."

. "Deal."

"JASPER," Jessica Booth yelled out to her husband in their bedroom bathroom, shaving before bed.

"Yes." Jasper peeped around the corner with the razor still in his hand and shaving cream on his face.

"Baby, did you see Jasmine's face when we were making the wedding plans?"

"I did, and at one point, I almost wanted to cry. I assumed she felt the same thing I felt when I found out that I wouldn't be able to walk her down the aisle."

"So, you're finally admitting that it hurt you not be able to walk your baby girl down the aisle?"

"Jessica, I know that I'm not supposed to favor one child over the others. I also know that the boys need their daddy too. Especially when they are making the decision to become a husband. But, there is something different about giving your daughter away. I know Vance is a good boy. Well...man. I also can look at my baby girl's eyes and see how happy he's making her. But..." Jasper hesitated.

"But what, baby?"

"But, I kind of was looking forward to one day handing her over in front of all of our family and friends looking on and feeling like I was losing the best gift you could have ever given me. Nevertheless, while at the same time eagerly feeling like now, someone has to finally love my baby as Christ loves His church."

"That's deep, Jasper."

"Yeah, but I won't dwell on what didn't happen. At least Vance asked me could he have my daughter's hand in marriage before they married. You know what, Jessica, I respect that young man. He's a good guy."

"He really is. I marvel at how God just united their family with ours by more than friendship."

"And it happened so quick. Girl, that Christmas gala did more than bless those babies. You put together a moment that heaven had already ordained, and that's when you know that you were led by the Spirit to do something. 'Cause when it happens, God shows up and changes some things."

"Well, He changed a lot of things that night, and I'm praising Him with my whole heart for what He's getting ready to do."

Jasper dried his hands and came towards Jessica.

"Come here, girl." He pulled his wife into his arms. "I haven't said this in a long time. 'I'm so proud of you.' You have gone above trees and mountains to make sure this family stays on the solid foundation."

"And you've made sure that foundation is Jesus. So, just as proud as you are of me, Jasper Booth, Sr., I'm just as proud of you."

Jasper bear-hugged his wife.

The smell of her hair, warmth, and softness of her body caused his body to react.

"Somebody's waking up."

"Girl, I've been awake since I saw you walking the halls of Booker T. Washington High School in that plaid skirt and white flowered-collar shirt. I loved you back then, but now, I love you with a love that has withstood the enemy's tests."

Jessica laughed. "Hallelujah."

"He's worthy of our praise, Jessica."

"Yes, He is," she agreed and embraced his kiss.

Jessica moaned. *He's going to be blown away when I surprise him. Jasper, you don't know it, but God is redeeming the task.*

CHAPTER 18

Kane laid his head back on his pillow and folded his hands behind his head. Staring at the rotating ceiling fan, he took a deep breath. He cringed at the thought of Veronica telling him that she wouldn't marry him at the surprise wedding, but even her no would mean she's talking to him, and that was a start.

She'd been gone for two full days and hadn't even sent a text.

Maybe this, too, was a part of his punishment for throwing that expensive phone. But in the heat of his anger, he was known to do some downright stupid things. Maybe it was the nepotism he'd learned first-hand from Jasper that came along with being a man—or was it *egotism*?

Either way, it had cost him separation from Veronica.

Buzz. Buzz.

He heard the buzzing of his cell phone, which was the notification that he had a text message. Kane turned his body slightly and picked up his phone, rolling back to his position.

Kane, this is Selena. Veronica loves you, but she feels like you blew up and all because she was suggesting that you all only get together when others are around. She never wanted you guys to break up. Look, we will be leaving as soon as the graveside funeral is over. Please don't tell her I text you. But please let me know that you got the text.

"Wow," he screamed.

His mother had warned him, in all your getting, get an understanding. And once again, he'd allowed an assumption to cause him to hang up on Veronica.

How ignorant could I have been?

He sighed and then decided to text Selena back.

Thanks for texting Selena. I've been wondering if you guys were okay. For real, I thought she was trying to break up with me, and I went crazy. Man, did I make a complete butt out of myself. I even threw my phone and broke it, so if she tried calling, I couldn't get the call. Just ridiculous. Look, take care of her for me. And as soon as you get return the city, please text me to find out where to bring her. We're planning a huge surprise. I just pray she doesn't tell me no.

He laid the phone on his chest in case Selena texted back.

Now he felt evermore like a first-class idiot.

"All she was doing was trying to keep both of us from making the wrong decision, and I just flipped out."

Then he heard the buzz again.

I will text you as soon as we land in Shreveport. Whatever the surprise is, you just better make sure it's huge. Elaborate. Gigantic. Enormous. Extraordinary. Because you, my brother are under the dog house. Not in it, but under it.

Kane laughed. He could just hear Selena in his head. *Thanks, Selena, cuz I owe you big. I promise it's going to be a surprise like she's never had before. And please, make sure your hair and face are already on point. Love you.*

Selena texted back, *Love you too, Kane. Now I'm excited.*

❦

SELENA THOUGHT BETTER of going to the house alone with Damon. She hadn't had sex in months, and being closed in with a man talking like he was talking was setting herself up for fornication. God had really been too good to her for her to sin against her own self. So she played it safe and stayed right there with Veronica.

She could see the pain in Veronica's eyes and had tried to make her call Kane, but she'd refused.

One thing about them, when their minds were made up, nothing could penetrate their resolve. She did what any good cousin or friend would do, she texted Kane.

Selena waited well until Veronica was in the shower, and then she picked up her phone. She didn't want to risk Veronica asking her if she was texting Damon, and lying to her. As soon as she typed the period at the end of *excited* and laid her phone on the table, Veronica opened the bathroom door.

Selena blew out a deep breath.

"What's the matter?" Veronica asked her.

"Nothing. Girl, did you hear Damon?"

"Did I. Selena, ole boy isn't giving up on being your boo without a straight-up fight."

"He had me crying like somebody had stolen my best candy bar."

Veronica laughed. "I saw you. I was in the backseat, chica."

"What the heck am I going to do?"

"Let that man love you, and you participate until you love him back."

"Vee, girl, but for real, I thought I was going crazy when I would see him looking at me. I was like: he looking at me like I'm a biscuit and he's a dog. Of course, anyone who has a homeboy who would cake on his wife is just that. So, I had to tell myself I didn't like him."

"But you did?"

"Girl, that dude is so handsome and, Vee, he can dance like he's been dancing all his life. When we were on vacation, I don't know how the two of us ended up salsa dancing, but he was turning me on. I had to hide my face, so Rufus wouldn't see my shame."

"I love a man who can dance, Selena. And Kane. That boy can dance his butt off. I think that's one of the reasons I fell so hard for him. But none of that matters now."

"Vee, who you fooling? You love that man, and he loves you. You just need to get back home and talk like for real. Talk. And if hanging up in your face makes you that angry, tell him. He doesn't know that because y'all never argued."

"You're right."

"I know I'm right. You're an amateur at this dating mess, and I'm a mess all the way around."

"You're my mess, and if you act like God has given you favor, you'll be Damon's mess too."

THE FUNERAL

Selena waited on Damon to pick up her, Abuela, and Veronica. She had been given strict instructions from Chief Linnear that all three of them were to wear the bulletproofed vests he'd delivered to Abuela's. He'd also told them to wait for Damon, who would pick up them and Rufus' mother, Catilina.

Not only was she ready to get this ordeal behind her, but to completely forget the life she'd be leaving behind. As she buried Rufus, it was her intent to conceal all her unforgiveness and hatred towards him.

She'd be moving on.

"He's here," her Abuela yelled.

"Coming," Selena and Veronica yelled in unison.

"Are you ready?" Veronica asked.

"I'm as ready as I can be," she responded with a smirk.

"If God be for you, Selena, who or what can be against you? He's going to see you through this day and every day. I promise."

Selena wrapped her arms around Veronica. "Thanks, cousin. I needed that."

When they met in the living room, Damon stood dressed as a limo driver. Selena wouldn't have recognized him if she'd met him in another space. She understood it was just as important he remained hidden as it was his job to protect her. Yet, a part of her wanted him beside her.

As the women walked out of the house, while he held open the door, Damon whispered to Selena, "Good morning, beautiful."

She only nodded, but the smile that reached her eyes could not be hidden if she wanted it.

They each got in the car, and he closed the door behind them. Veronica and Selena took the rear backseat so that their abuela and Catilina could sit in the middle. When they pulled up at Catilina's, Selena took in a deep breath. All of Rufus' cousins and family were gathered. Some of them looked as ruthless as Rufus's acts were towards her.

"Good Morning," Catilina spoke as she climbed into the limousine.

"Good Morning. Catilina, it's so good to see you," Marita said, touching her gently on the arm.

"It's good to see all of you. Especially my daughter, who has not come to see me since arriving." Catilina turned towards the back to see Selena's face. "Don't cry, pretty girl. I didn't mean to offend you."

"It's not you, Mother Catilina," Selena called her by the name she'd given her when she first met her. "I just... I'm just full this morning."

"This is not easy for any of us, sweet girl. We all know that my son was not the man God designed him to be, but my prayer is that somehow our dear Father gave him room to repent."

As tears rolled down Selena's face, she sat up and touched Catilina on the arm. She had so much compassion for Catilina, and she truly loved her with everything in her.

"Catilina, I will always be your daughter for the rest of my life, and one day, you will be the grandmother of my children. Nosotras solos familia (*we are family*)."

"Gracias (thank you). He decidido ir contigo hija (*I've decided to go with you, daughter*)."

"Aleluya (hallelujah). Gracias (thank you). Te honraré como madre y te cuidaré (*I will honor you as mother and take care of you*)." Selena touched Catilina on the arm.

By now, all four women were crying, but Selena could see the smile in Damon's eyes as he looked into the rearview mirror, and her eyes caught his. Although he had confessed his feelings towards her, this was the perfect time to show him that she came as a package deal. If he could not accept Catilina, then he could not have her. She would never leave her.

When they pulled into the graveyard, there were policemen and gangsters everywhere. A quick spirit of fear washed over Selena, but by the time Damon grasped her arm to escort her from the car, it all vanished.

He was her protector.

And his touch told her everything she needed to know.

The priest stood before them, "Estamos reunidos aquí hoy para celebrar la vida de nuestro querido hermano (*We are gathered here today to celebrate the life of our dear brother*). Dios ha visto conveniente tomarlo, pero sus buenas obras vivirán (*God has saw fit to take him, but his good works will live on*). Vamos a orar (*Let's pray*).

"Bien (*okay*)," the guests responded.

"Padre nuestro que estás en el cielo santificado sea tu nombre. Tu reino viene tu se hará en la tierra como lo es en el cielo. Danos hoy nuestro pan de cada día. Y perdónanos nuestras ofensas como nosotros perdonamos a los que nos ofenden. Y no nos dejes caer en la tentación, pero líbranos del mal. Porque tuyo es el reino y el poder y la gloria, para siempre. Amén. (*Our Father which art in heaven hallowed be thy name. Thine kingdom come, thine will be done, on earth as it is in heaven. Give us this day our daily bread. And forgive us our trespasses as we forgive those who trespass against us. And lead us not into temptation, but deliver us from evil. For thine is the kingdom and the power and the glory, forever. Amen*)."

"Amen," the crowd repeated.

"Ahora tendremos una canción de Veronica (*We will now have a song by Veronica*)."

"Buenos días," Veronica said as she stood with the microphone in her hand. She was so nervous because she was about to sing a song that was dear to her abuela's heart.

The hymn she would attempt to sing, "Ave Maria," originated from

Ellen's Third Song, written by Franz Schubert in 1825. It was at the request of Selena that she sang this moving prayer.

Veronica closed her eyes and began to sing, "Ave Maria, Gratia plena, Maria, Gratia plena, Maria, Gratia plena, Ave, Ave, Dominus, Dominus tecum. Benedicta tu in mulieribus, Et benedictus, Et benedictus frutcus ventris, ventris tu, Jesus. Ave Maria! (*Hail Mary, full of grace, Mary, full of grace, Mary, full of grace, Hail, Hail, the Lord, The Lord is with thee. Blessed art thou among women, and blessed, Blessed is the fruit of thy womb, Thy womb, Jesus. Hail Mary!*)"

Ave Maria, mater Dei, Ora pro nobis peccatoribus, Ora, ora pro nobis; Ora, ora pro nobis peccatoribus, Nunc, et in hora mortis, In hora mortis nostrae. In hora, hora mortis nostrae, In hora mortis nostrae. Ave Maria! Amen. (*Holy Mary, Mother of God, Pray for us sinners, Pray, pray for us; Pray for us sinners, Now, and at the hour of our death, The hour of our death. The hour, the hour of our death, The hour of our death. Hail Mary! Amen.*)"

There was not a dry eye when Veronica finished. Even the hardest of gangsters connected to Rufus by blood was crying and swiping their eyes.

After Veronica's rendition of the song, Selena took to the microphone.

"Catilina y yo les doy las gracias a todos por venir (*Catilina and I thank you for coming*). Es nuestra oración que recuerden el bien que hizo Rufus (*It is our prayer that you remember the good that Rufus did*). Que el Padre os bendiga a todos. En el nombre del Padre, del Hijo y del Espíritu Santo (*May the Father bless you all, in the name of the Father, Son, and Holy Spirit*)."

Selena grabbed Catilina by the hand. The two walked away from the casket hand in hand with Veronica and Marita following behind them. The police band played "Taps." Then, guns were fired in salute of a fallen officer. The fact he hadn't fallen by the hands of anyone except himself bothered Selena. But she was thankful the Lord had seen fit to allow Rufus to have a dignified send-off. If only she could be quieted in heart concerning what she considered was his coward's way out of trouble.

When they made it to their car, Catilina turned to face Selena,

"Selena, Dios ha cubierto sus acciones porque hizo algo bueno. (*Selena, God has covered his deeds because he did do some good*)."

"Gracias, Catilina (*Thank you, Catilina*)." Selena kissed his mother on the cheek. Catilina didn't know it, but in an instant, she'd calmed Selena's racing heart.

"God really does answer prayers," Veronica whispered.

"Yes, He does." Selena kissed her cousin's cheek.

CHAPTER 19

T hings were moving quick.

Jessica had more than fifty hired helpers to make sure the tents were up, and everything that could be dressed was dressed. A seventy-two-hundred square foot tent was decorated as a lounging section where most of the guests would await the start of the ceremony. This tent had a door that led to the one-hundred-eighty by three-hundred-sixty foot custom-made tent. It was large enough for the formal-dinner-styled seating, five bar areas, ten buffet tables, and ten waiter stations. You could walk out of a door from this dinner tent into a huge sixty by one hundred and twenty-foot canvas which was equipped with a stage for the band, a DJ booth, and a glass dance floor that housed koi fish in all colors and shades that bore the initials J-B & K in the middle covered in florescent lighting.

If Jessica could have stayed in that particular tent for life, she would have. It almost felt like walking on water.

She had pulled no stops at making sure all of their guests were suffi-ciently accommodated and would have the time of their lives. There were four photographers hired for the wedding ceremony alone, and two extra would fill in for the reception and dancing.

One thing was sure, she needed to be able to have every memory they could capture for five wedding photo books. She'd decided to make sure that both Kane's maternal and paternal grandparents received a wedding book, and both couples, and definitely, she and Valerie. Two of the proudest women on earth.

The good thing was that she and Jasper were killing two weddings with one massive production that would be fancier than the Christmas in the Field event, but also as extravagant as J.J. and Jade's wedding. Everyone was doing exactly what she had needed of them, and no one was complaining.

The only hard thing was keeping Jasper and Jasmine from knowing this was also for her and the chance he thought he'd missed.

And Jessica was so proud of her daughter-in-love Jade, who made sure that every dress was unique and that the entire wedding party was fit and ready. The only thing was making sure the videographers were on deck and hiding for the apology.

Jessica didn't know how things would pan out, but as long as the Lord was in it, they could only win.

If every detail had gone as planned, Chief Linnear would make sure the girls and Catilina caught the first private plane to Shreveport, and Marita would be on a flight with Chief Linnear, his wife, daughter, and Damon. And if the plan was being carried out, the girls should be landing in another thirty minutes. Jessica went to the center of the yard and used the microphone to make her announcement.

"Guests, we have about thirty minutes, and the bride will be landing. It will take thirty minutes to get her from the airport to here, so please enjoy the hors d'oeuvres."

"Yes," some of the crowd yelled, while others clapped.

Everyone who was considered the elite of Louisiana and Christianity would attend this epic event. There would be two Booth family members coming together in marriage with two Kimbrel's, a rarity, but yet divinity at work. You didn't have to pay to get a ticket in, but your gifts were expected to match what you would have paid considering the types of events Jessica Booth put on.

But even if you came empty-handed, Jessica Booth's desire was to give you an experience that God ordained for you to have. Two weddings, a gift in itself.

Jessica spotted her true love standing over, staring at all the commotion going on. She walked quickly, hoping that he didn't move.

She touched him on his back, and without even seeing her, he asked, "What do you need love?"

"How did you know it was me?"

"I felt you from afar, and the closer you got to me, the more I smelt your scent."

"You..."

"Yes, me, the man who is always so proud of you. I'm so honored that God chose me to cover you." He pulled his wife from behind him to the front of him, to look in her eyes.

"Me too, love," she replied.

"Jessica, you have truly outdone yourself. Girl, you surprise me daily. I'm just..." Jasper shook his head.

"The man God sent to protect, cover, love, cherish, respect, and spend your money o: Me."

Jasper laughed a hearty laugh. "Exactly. And I hope you know that there is nothing I won't do for you. You will always have spot number two in my heart on lock."

"Amen, because if you ever gave me spot number one, I'd have to leave you. And as long as God remains first in your life, you'll always be in mine. I love you, Jasper Booth, Sr."

"I love you, Jessica Booth."

"Now, go put on your tux."

"Yes, madam. I was wondering why I couldn't just wear my suit, though."

"Because I want you to look better than any man on our property, including the groom."

"That's my girl, always wanting her man to outshine the rest."

"You better know it. And don't ever forget it."

"Yes, madam, and I'm good at following orders because following wifey orders by day, leads to happy nights."

"They sure do." Jessica winked and blushed.

CHAPTER 20

Veronica helped Selena gather her baggage. Once they had everything that belonged to them, they walked to exit the private plane with Catilina following closely behind them. Selena was in awe of how their friends would lend even their most expensive possessions. It was as though nothing to them mattered more than helping a friend in need.

As the assistant pilot helped them down the stairs, Selena shook her head as Veronica waited at the bottom for her and Catilina.

"I know what you're thinking. The Booths are privileged, but they're not poisoned by it."

"I don't know how you knew it, but I definitely thought this is like, wow."

"I felt the same way, then I realized they view everything they have as a blessing. Their greatest aspiration is to be a blessing to others with the abundance of what God has given them. You know, I used to feel like you gave people only what you didn't want anymore. Through the Jackson-Booth clan," Veronica made quotation marks with her fingers, "you give whatever helps to meet the need."

"That sounds so liberating," Selena said, then grabbed Catilina by the hand.

"It's just what you've done for me, Selena. I feel like the modern-day Naomi who's following Ruth instead of Ruth following her." Catilina laughed.

"Your relationship simply shows that when God has a plan, even when the devil thinks he's doing his best work, it will still work out for our good." Veronica opened the door to the airport so they could pass through to get to her car.

Selena nodded, "You're right about that, Vee. Now, before we go home, we have a stop to make."

"I should have known you had somewhere to be because you got too snatched for a plane ride home. You and Catilina."

"Chica, I stay snatched," Catilina used her finger and her head movement to solidify her point.

"I know that's real, mother. Would you tell Vee that Burns women are beauties."

"She doesn't have to tell me, Selena, because I'm looking at you two beauties live and in living color. Now, where am I taking you, women?"

"We need to go to Jessica's house. She's making sure Catilina is affirmed into Louisiana living."

"That figures. My mother-in-love is a hoot," Veronica laughed.

"Oh, so does that mean you've forgiven, Kane? And, you're still planning on becoming his wife?"

"I didn't say all of that. Although Jessica won't lose her status even if he loses his. I absolutely adore her, and she'll always be in my life. Just like Catilina will always be in yours."

"Praise the Lord! Glory to His name," Catilina praised.

The Spirit dropped in her mind, "Glory to His Name."

Veronica started singing, "Glory to His name."

Selena and Catilina joined in, "Glory to His name, Glory to His name, precious name, There to my heart was the blood applied; Glory to His name."

Catilina continued, "A su nombre gloria! A su nombre gloria! Allí en mi corazón estaba la sangre aplicada, A su nombre gloria!"

Both Selena and Veronica laughed because one thing was for sure,

Catilina nor Marita weren't going to allow them to lose the passion for their heritage.

⚜

"OKAY, Marita, and company are pulling in the parking lot. If I'm correct, Veronica, Selena, and Catilina should be arriving shortly. I need all of you to stay behind the fence, and when it's time, I will make sure you all don't miss any part of the wedding. Kane, I need you to be waiting in the front and make sure to walk Veronica right into the house. I'll be waiting to take Catilina and then give Selena directives. People to pull this off, we must be quiet and move quickly."

"Understood!" Valerie yelled, causing Jessica to snicker.

If anyone else was as excited as Jessica, it was Valerie. She was just as scared too. Neither of them knew what Veronica was feeling, and if she decided not to marry Kane, it could derail the entire plan. But both did what any waiting mother would do; they secretly prayed.

The videographers already had the cameras set up and ready, and as soon as Kane clapped his hands, they knew to start taping. The outside photographers moved about capturing the guests and decorations. The two set for the in house activities were doing their jobs to perfection.

By the time Veronica pulled in the circular drive, the set was prepped and ready for action.

⚜

KANE MET Veronica as she got out of the car.

He spoke to both Selena and Catilina but asked Veronica if she would go with him.

Veronica didn't fuss or fight as he thought she would and allowed him to lead her into his parents' den.

"Vee, I'm so, so, sorry. I was so wrong on so many different levels. I made the wrong accusation, which led to the wrong decision, and this has nearly cost me the love of my life. Please say you're still the love of my life."

115

"Kane," she whispered.

"I can't live without you, Vee. I went to counseling and realized that as soon as you said the word separate, I felt anxiety shoot through me. I also realized that I'd secretly been holding on to the neglect I felt from my parents leaving me and then dying. To hear you—"

"Kane," Veronica interrupted him. "I was only going to suggest that we separate from the private dinners. You know, include Selena and our parents on our date nights. Things were getting a bit too much for me to handle. I love you, but I wanted to make sure to stick with the vow I made to God. We said no sex before marriage but had I experienced too many more nights of you rubbing my feet, I would have raped you."

Kane laughed. "Vee, you can't be serious."

"Yes. I am. I was losing control, and I promise I would have snatched all of your clothes off had Selena not called me that night."

"Girl, you? I did all of that crazy stuff because you were getting weak?"

"Yes. And you didn't let me finish talking before you hung up on me. I called you back several times, and you wouldn't answer your phone. That's when I made the decision to just leave."

"Baby, I threw my phone against the wall, and it shattered. I was devastated because I thought you were breaking things off. Man, what a big fool I've made of myself. Can you forgive me?"

"I can, but only if you promise never to ever hang up the phone in my face. That was so rude, but now I understand why you did it."

"Baby, I just felt like I was losing you. I wanted you as much as you wanted me that night. I was even glad Selena called. I didn't want you to think bad of me."

"Well, we were in the same boat together."

"The boat I pray we'll stay in for the rest of our lives. Veronica, I will not spend another day on earth without you as my wife. Will you marry me right now?"

"Now? Look at me. I can't, like this."

"Now, you know me. I'd never compromise your dream for the sake of my own desires. All you have to do is say yes."

"Yes," Veronica said, and before she could say anything else, her eyes were covered. Someone picked her up to carry her to only God knew where.

"Kane, Kane," she called out.

"Do you trust me, Vee?"

"I trust you," Veronica said.

"If you do, trust the process and know that I've got you, and from this moment forward, I will never let you go."

"Okay," she cried through tears that struggled to flow from behind the mask.

Kane kissed her hand as Vance held her in his arms. "The next time you see me, I'll be waiting for you, my love."

CHAPTER 21

As Jade, Jasmine, Selena, and Jamecia dressed Veronica in the one of a kind Jourdain's design created for Veronica, they tried to calm her nerves. Kane had Jamecia design the exact replica of the red gown he previously bought for her. Opting instead for a rose-gold colored wedding gown.

All of the women gasped at how beautiful Veronica was, and she cried behind her still-hidden eyes.

"Stop crying, Vee. You're making all of us cry," Jade teased.

"I'm just so happy. I am too happy to be scared. Can I take off the blindfold?"

"Not until we're finished," Jamecia quickly responded. "I want to be completely finished when you take off your blinders.

The ladies kept working until Valerie came into the room.

And as soon as Valerie opened the door, she and her mother Marita instantly released the waterworks any mother and grandmother would upon seeing an angel.

Jasmine took Valerie's hand and instructed her to unveil Veronica as soon as they left the room, and Valerie did as told.

"Oh, Mom. Look at me," Veronica squealed.

"I see you, baby. Your daddy would have been so happy to see you now, but I know he's here. He lives through you and through Vance."

"He does, Mom." Veronica embraced her mother.

"I'm so happy to be here with my girls," Marita said as she smiled, glaring at Valerie and Veronica. And before she could move beyond the sentiments of what this moment represented, Vashti and Selena entered the room. Five women, five hearts, all connected in love but still had one substantial undiscussed situation in between them. And Marita refused to allow the unspoken ordeal to destroy what was taking place right here, right now.

"I'm so grateful that God has allowed me to see both of my girls and my granddaughters in the same room and here with me. And Valerie, Quiero empezar de nuevo con usted. ¿Me perdona? (*I want to start over with you. Will you forgive me?*)"

"Mamá, ya te he perdonado (*Momma, I have already forgiven you*)."

All five of the ladies were crying because this was the reunion their family needed. So many more words needed to be spoken, but now was definitely not the time. The focus needed to be on Veronica, and Valerie had sense enough to know and understand that nothing mattered except Veronica.

It was a mother's love at work.

And God's hand of mercy rested upon.

JESSICA HANDLED BUSINESS. She moved about the yard, trying to tie up loose ends and make sure all the hands involved worked at transforming the yard into a five-hundred-seat outdoor sanctuary. From the curb to the last landmark to distinguish their sixty acres of land from their neighbors, their entire yard was already sanctified as God's. But anytime they were having something unique, Jessica called forth her prayer warriors to walk the land and pray.

This week instead of walking, they'd jumped on eight four-wheelers containing two women each, and drove, stopped, and prayed until they had covered all sixty acres.

Where the spirit of the Lord is, there is liberty. And nothing could refute that point. In that liberty, Jessica fulfilled the wishes of her husband and the dream wedding for her children.

Jessica stopped for a photographic memory moment of the complete transformation of her home.

The first thing she noticed was the same fleur-de-lis water fountains used in J.J.'s wedding, as they now stood at the top of the walkway as an entrance to the aisle. She smiled at the four commercial noiseless fans—blowing air in all directions—that Veronica's boss, Dwight Esplanade, designed for the occasion. *God is so good that He'll allow people to create for your cause.*

The glass flooring that held koi fish just like the dance floor ran from the back to the front of the aisles that ended in a twenty by eighty feet glass platform stage that contained rose-gold and clear-colored koi fish, under a gazebo large enough to shade the complete wedding party and the two couples from the sun. There were two individual ten by ten foot spaces elevated higher than the base platform for each couple to have their own private platform; and an extended area in the center of both for Pastor Roderick Strong to officiate.

The gazebo was wrapped in white roses, and the backdrop featured a huge K and J-B in rose-gold flowers. It was absolutely gorgeous to see nature and grace brought into the same space. For Jessica, the fish took on a deeper meaning.

The koi fish represented perseverance in adversity and strength of purpose. For Vance and Jasmine, they had persevered through the worst of times and the most traumatic circumstance. Kane and Veronica had also shown their ability to continue through the Rufus situation, but the strength of purpose God designed for them went far beyond their love.

He had orchestrated their lives through loss and through being able to forgive. Their purpose as individuals was so dynamic, but in two as one, it would be life-changing. Jessica believed—for these two couples—today was only a fraction of what God had in store for them.

Jessica instructed her head usher that after everything was completely done, the guests would take a seat in the makeshift wedding chapel. The orchestra had already begun serenading the guests with musical selections rendered by songstress Jacqueline Antwine. There was nothing like a true worshipper who could usher people into God's presence with pure angelic singing.

Guests patiently stood enjoying drinks, and some were praising God as others were enthralled in the excellency of the vocals. For sure, God's Spirit was invited for such an occasion as this. After she was certain nothing else could be done, Jessica made her way inside to make the surprise that awaited her husband and daughter.

She peeked in at the bridesmaids in beautiful creme-colored gowns, holding the gorgeous blush and rose gold flowers designed by Dobrielle's.

Jessica smiled. "Ladies, we're almost ready to get this show on the road. Thank you all for being a part of this wonderful day."

"Okay," they answered.

Then she found Jasmine in a room with Jade, and she helped put the finishing touches on her baby. After she finished, Jessica closed the door and journeyed into her bedroom. First, she needed to just take a seat. And after she'd calmed her spirit, she quickly took a shower and dressed in her creme-colored gown.

Jessica's mind drifted to her conversation with Jasmine as she and Jade helped her to dress.

"Mom, you certainly made my gown just as beautiful as Veronica's. I don't want to outdo the bride."

"Girl, you're my daughter, and if you're going to stand with Veronica, I want you to be just as darling."

"You know I can't argue with that, but I really want this day to be about her."

"Jasmine, because your heart is so pure, God is going to bless you, my love."

"Thanks, Mom. You've taught me that being the center of attention never comes at the cost of us stealing someone else's light. This is Veronica's light."

"I love you, my sweet girl. I also love how you have eagerly embraced your new sisters. Our family is just expanding, and I'm so thankful."

"Me too, Mom," Jasmine responded. Tears rolled down her cheeks.

"Mom, why are you crying already?"

"I'm so happy, Jasmine. My first baby is getting married, and all my babies are here with me."

"Mother J, we need you to hold it together."

"Okay, Jade. Momma is trying," Jessica answered, knowing well why Jade was cautioning her. She'd held on too long to lose the secret because of emotions.

"Jasmine so you won't be nervous today, I want you to wear my blue diamonds anklet. It was given to me by my grandmother, and it helped me when I stood to sing at the last convocation. I believe it's going to help you today."

"Jade, thank you, sissy. I love you, and since all I'll be doing is holding Veronica's flowers, I'm sure I'll have more than enough strength."

Jade kissed Jasmine's cheek. *"You will, Jas. I love you, and you know me and what I believe."*

"One can never have enough strength," Jasmine and Jade said together and laughed.

Jessica turned Jasmine to the mirror.

"Baby, you are beautiful," she fixed one of Jasmine's curls and made sure her tiara was straightened.

"I get it from my momma," Jasmine responded and bent to kiss her mother.

Knock. Knock.

Jessica's thought broke when she heard a rap at her door.

"Come in," she answered.

"Sis, everything is so beautiful, and Veronica is ready now. I've sent all of my family down."

"Perfect, Valerie. Now is Vance walking her down the aisle?"

"No. Girl, she wants her new father to do it. And you should have seen the look on James' face when she asked him. That pretty brown-skinned man got more handsome to me at that moment."

"I know, huh. Just to see how he loves your children, right?"

"That, and also, to see how he looked at Veronica as if she came from his very own loins. Girl, it nearly sucked the breath out of me. Loving a man who loves your babies, who's honored to play the role of a father is the Lord on display."

"Oh, yes. How the Father moves into the role of our Daddy. Abba

Father, for His children of adoption. Jesus!" Jessica screamed. "I felt that, Val."

"So did I. Girl, you gonna start a fire up in this here room that water can't put out. Come on, let me zip you up."

"Thanks, honey. I told both boys to stand on their box, and I'll have Jasper to walk Jasmine in first, and then James can walk Veronica in last. That way, Jasmine still thinks she's playing matron of honor until she hits that platform, and Vance is waiting on her."

"Girl, you guys are serious on this surprising stuff. You just be on that front row so you can wipe her and Jasper's tears."

"I know, right?"

"Okay, you look good. Pin that piece of your hair up, and let's get these two handsome Booth men to walk us down their aisles first."

"I'm behind you, sis. Hold on, let me put a little of Jasper's favorite perfume on my neck."

"Uhh, so tonight won't just be a honeymoon for these couples, will it?"

"Not if I can help it. He has to repay me for this big surprise and trust me, sister is ready."

"I feel you, sis. I'm so glad age ain't nothing but a number."

"And I'm glad I didn't lose my ability to satisfy my man as the numbers increased."

"Won't He do it?" Valerie slapped Jessica's hand.

"Yes, He will." Jessica clapped hers back.

CHAPTER 22

The music change suggested that it was time for the grandparents and aunts to be escorted to their seats. The band played a rendition of "Ava Maria." After they were all seated, the orchestra started playing "Moonlight Sonata" by Beethoven.

It had been the first song Jasper played for Jessica on their first date. Something about the melody caused Jessica to feel like the Lord Himself was showing Beethoven how music met love, yielding to the most extravagant of musical notes in the hearts of those ordained to come together.

As Jasper walked his wife down the aisles behind Valerie and James, he squeezed her hand with the gentlest of squeezes, and she, of course pressed his back. And when he set her at her seat, she whispered, "Now, go get your girl and try not to cry."

Jasper kissed his wife and smiled, but he wasn't sure what she meant by that last part. He and James stood watching as the first couple prepared to walk down the aisles. It was Jasper Jr. and Jade. Jade kissed him, and he noticed his daughter-in-love wore a microphone. He mouthed to James, "It's on now."

As soon as the ushers held open the beautiful cream drapes separating the audience's view from who would come through, Jade began to sing Our Holy Trinity.

♪♪A love like ours,

Has stood the test of times.

There's one thing I know

What we have is pure divine.

A love like ours,

Is a pure and special kind

The next thing I know

What we have is love divine.

God brought us together, we can handle stormy weather.

Me for you, you for me, it's a holy affinity.

God will keep us together, with Him it only gets better.

Me for you, you for me, with Him our Holy Trinity.

God brought us to me for you, you for me, with Him our Holy Trinity.

God brought us through me for you, you for me, with Him our Holy Trinity.♪♪

⊙⊱⊙

WHEN JADE GOT to the middle of the aisles, everyone who had known all these couples endured was crying. After the four flower girls, it was time for the first bride to walk down the aisle. Neither Jasper nor Jasmine still had a clue why she was escorted or why he was escorting her. But when they opened the curtains, and everyone stood up, the people could tell by the way they looked at one another, it had dawned on them what was taking place.

Jasmine focused her eyes and saw the man of her dreams. He stood on a platform to the left and her brother to the right. Then she looked to her side at her father, who was filled with emotions himself.

Steven Marshall, the church music director, was now on the grand piano and the Faith Temple Cathedral's ensemble, along with the orchestra, and with Jacqueline Antwine, as their guest started singing "God's Picture of Joy" written by Jade and composed by Jasper Sr.

♪♪It's not by happenstance, we were brought together
You would cover me, and I would honor you
It's not a coincidence that you would vow to love me
I will cherish you, and you would pray us through
There's nothing magical in this love we have, no.
It's nothing ordinary, and no we're never settling
But what it is, What this is,
It something spiritual,
Divine will unfold
A rib that found it's place,
God's amazing grace
The answer to our prayer
A plan formed in heaven
Two hearts that beat as one,
God's picture of joy.♪♪

Jasper Sr. instantly recognized the song Jade brought to him to put music to. They'd worked on it for three straight hours and although he loved the lyrics, he had no idea why Jade was rushing him and why it was so crucial for her to nail it.

Now he knew.

Jasper's eyes met his daughter-in-love, and through tears, he smiled. He felt Jasmine trembling, and he stopped mid-aisle and turned to his daughter.

"I love you, Jasmine. I am so honored to walk you to the man you love. And if you never hear this from anyone else, I know what you have with Vance is truly God's picture of joy. Now, Daddy's going to dry your eyes, so we can make this the best pictures they'll get today."

Jasmine snickered. 'Cause all it took was for her daddy to boost her head up, and she'd move mountains to make him proud.

And as if he read her thoughts, Jasper said, "I could not be more proud of you. You heard God concerning that man." Jasper looked towards Vance. "And nothing I or anyone else said moved you from your stance. I taught you to obey God at all costs, and you proved to God and me that you would. You've been faithful over a few things, my baby, and He's going to make you ruler over many."

"I love you, Daddy."

"I love you more. Now, come on 'cause that boy up there crying like I'm talking you out of this."

Jasmine laughed and leaned in to kiss her favorite guy on the cheek.

Jasper Sr. proudly walked his daughter to the stairs to the stage, and Vance came down to receive his wife. He hugged Jasper Sr., took Jasmine by her hand, and walked her to their personal stage to their huge king and queen chairs.

⚜

Jasper Booth Sr. took his seat and pulled his wife, Jessica, into his arms. This woman. He looked down at her and shook his head. How could he have ever put himself in a position to almost lose the best thing God could have ever blessed him with? How could he have allowed the wrong decision to almost tear his home apart? How could he have been so foolish and self-centered until his only care had been what he wanted?

Every answer would only yield space for one word.

A word that he hated. A word he whooped his children for saying. A word the Bible told him never to call a man, but he found himself in a position where the only word that would explain the foolishness he'd done for fit for describing his lack of consideration, lousy judgment, lusting, and proud behavior...stupid. Down right stupid.

He could see tears running down Jessica's face and knew the whole scene that she had helped recreate for him made her just as emotional as he was. How did she know it would mean so much for him to walk his only girl down the aisle? How did she make this plan and keep it from him for all of these days? *How in the world did she do it?*

And it was then that Jasper realized: she indeed was the rib that found its place. She was the best part of God's divine will unfold for his life. Why waking up in the morning felt miraculous and lying in bed next to her at night felt like the safest place on earth.

Jasper leaned in and kissed her on the top of her head.

Then he bent his mouth at her ear. "I love you, Jessica, with every

128

ounce of my being, and you have made me five times and more the most blessed man on this earth. I honor you, my love, with all that's in me. I will never, for as long as we live, do anything to hurt you again. I know that if you could have left me, you would have. And to be honest, baby, you should have. But I'm so glad God told you to stay. You honored Him above how you felt and what you wanted, and that spoke volumes. Jessica, you're the reason I praise Him. I praise Him because He's God, He's good, and He's merciful. But I praise Him most because He blessed me to find the missing piece of me and put us together so that even we could not tear it apart."

Jessica was so full she could barely speak.

With all the strength she could muster, she looked at her one true love and said, "I am so in love with you, Jasper Booth Sr., and this is until death parts us."

Then the musical selection was over, and the music for the next bride was about to start.

CHAPTER 23

Veronica stood holding on to James' arm as if for dear life. She was still blindfolded and had yet to see herself. *I sure wish someone would take this mask off.* As if they heard her secret desire, someone took off the eye-cover. When she gained her focus and her eyes adjusted, she peered at the woman staring back at her in the mirror.

Her grimace caused James to pull her into him. "Don't cry, baby girl, you are just as beautiful in your heart as you are this day. Now, are you ready to take this victory walk?"

"Yes." She nodded her head but had no recourse for the tears. They ran down her cheek, and to her surprise, the makeup artist was right there to dab and touch-up everything that released water, including her nose.

"Thank you," Veronica told the young lady when she had finished. "Let's do this, Dad." And now it was James' turn to cry. He'd always wanted children of his own, but as fate would have it, that wasn't in God's plan. Now he had two grown children, but to him, they were the girl and boy he'd always prayed for. "Mister, now you don't cry." Veronica squeezed him.

"Okay. I'm good," James used his handkerchief to wipe his eyes and nose and then placed it back in his jacket pocket, "sounds like the music is beginning."

Veronica nodded, closed her eyes, and whispered a silent prayer as she heard the voice of her boss, Dwight Esplanade. She knew his singing voice even if they were in the midst of thousands of singers. He had a black-boy-gone-country sound, and she loved country music. As she and James walked through the now-opened drapes, Dwight sang words that would forever remind her of this day.

♪♫Sometimes, I don't always do what's right
I don't always make the best choice
Sometimes, I have to reconsider my ways
Have to ask the Lord to help me number my days
But today, I chose to let time standstill
To stay right here in God's perfect will
To remember you on this very day
To pledge my life, love, vow to stay
Forever and ever with you, this is where I wanna be.
Forever and ever with you, no longer I or me, it's we.
Forever and ever with you, with love, faith, and harmony.
Forever and ever with you, the Father, You, and Me.♪♫

As Veronica walked down the aisles, her eyes landed on Selena. Selena's smile caused her to trace her cousin's eyes. *Damon. He's already stolen her heart.* Veronica winked at Selena, who had abandoned Damon to smile at her.

Veronica turned her attention back to the words of the song and the man that awaited her hand.

♪♫Sometimes I say things that I shouldn't say
I don't always win sometimes I lose
Sometimes, I have to fall on my knees and pray
Have to ask the Lord please don't let me stray—ay
But today, I chose to let time standstill
To stay right here in God's perfect will
To remember you this our wedding day
To pledge my life, love, vow to stay.
Forever and ever with you, this is where I wanna be.

Forever and ever with you, no longer I or me, it's we.♪♫

When she made it to the bottom of the stairs that would lead her to Kane, James kissed her on the cheek and whispered, "You're going to be the perfect wife for nephew. I love you, my daughter."

She allowed the tears to cascade down her cheeks at the warm sentiments coming from James. The man who now took on the role of father to her and Vance. Someone who didn't understand the dynamics of their family would swear they were a bunch of weirdos. Veronica snickered thinking about an old saying folks adapted for cousins who crossed the line. Rooster, rooster, ginny, ginny, kinfolks stuff is as good as any.

But thank God, that nastiness didn't apply to them.

Explaining to others why Kane called her new father uncle would probably be a task but who cared. They knew the deal, and at this point, nothing else even mattered.

Kane gathered her hand safely in his. She followed him up the stairs and onto the platform built for the two of them.

"Greetings to each of you," Pastor Strong said while flipping through his little black book's pages.

"Who gives these beautiful women to be married to these men?"

"We do," both Jasper and James stood up from opposite sides of the room. The left side was filled with Jasmine and Kane's family and friends, and the other side with the family and friends of Veronica and Vance.

The room was filled with all types of ethnicities, cultures, and backgrounds, but the most important of all, love. There was so much love in the room until couples held on to one another, and those who were single wished God would open the portals of heaven to send them a love of their own.

As Kane and Vance extended a hand to help their bride from their seat, they each stood to face their bride as Pastor Roderick P. Strong delivered the preliminary vows.

"Now, I heard that each of you has your own vows to say to your bride. Is this correct?"

"Yes, sir," both Kane and Vance answered.

Pastor Strong nodded. "And likewise with the brides."

"No, sir," Jasmine looked to Veronica to confirm her fear.

The crowd and Pastor Strong laughed. Then he said, "Oh, that's right, these nuptials are a surprise to both of you, huh?"

"Yes, sir," they answered.

"I'm sure that the Holy Spirit will tell you exactly what to say. And, you've been together long enough to know how you both feel, right?"

This caused a broad smile to spread on both of their faces.

"So, we will start with Vance and Jasmine, and after you, Kane and Veronica, I will say a few more things. Is this okay with you all?"

"Yes," they all answered.

"Well, Vance, present your vows." Pastor Strong nodded his head.

Vance took both of Jasmine's hands in his after she handed her bouquet to Jade, "Jasmine, you have been all I've ever wanted in a wife and so much more than what I prayed for. The only regret I've ever had since the day you gave me your hand in marriage is that Mr. Jasper wasn't able to walk you down the aisle. This day, all of my regrets have now been resolved, and I take you, Jasmine, over and over, forever and always to be my loving wife. I promise to hold you close when you get scared, cover you when the world tries to harm you, protect you from anything that exalts itself above the knowledge of God, and love you as Christ has loved His church. I will never forsake you and, at the same time, stand guard to forsake anyone who tries to come between us. You are my reason for fighting to live, and will always be the first person I pray for. I am your husband, your covering in every matter, and if you allow me, I will prove to be your earthly king."

Jasmine motioned to wipe her tears, and Jade appeared dapping her sister's eyes and then returned to her matron of honor spot. Everyone laughed because it had seemed like a well-rehearsed part of a play. When the crowd stopped laughing, Jasmine smiled and then began.

"Vance, you are the reason for the smile, the miracle which has become an awakening to my soul. I honor you even now, as my earthly king, and I understand better the love my parents share. When I wake up, I tell the Lord, 'Thank You,' because I realize the blessing He's given me in you. I will love God with all of my heart, mind, and soul, but you, Vance, I'll love you more than I love myself. I promise to obey you as though you have the rule over me but help you as though it was purposed for me to do before our creation. I won't ever turn my back on you, and I will trust the process that God has planned for us. I give you my life, my love, and my womb until death due us apart."

No one could have stopped Vance from pulling Jasmine into his arms and holding her as if he had never held her before. And as they both cried, the guests, along with their parents, family, and friends, also cried. Steven queued the musicians, and they started playing "Open Heaven" as sung by gospel sensation, Maranda Curtis.

CHAPTER 24

Pastor Strong gave the worshippers time to worship as everyone, including the couples worshipped before the King, who wanted His appearance to be made known. Because indeed, the pair were both signs of God's miracles, signs, and wonders being performed in the earth.

The good thing was no one was owed any rent, and they could stay in the makeshift venue until God was good and finished.

Pastor Strong praised God a little more and then turned his attention towards the next couple.

"Are you all ready," he asked Kane and Veronica.

"Praise the Lord," Veronica shouted out, and the praise started all over again. It was as if her praise rippled, and in an instant, people began dancing as Steven led the musicians into Apostolic praise music.

Pastor Strong stood back watching God move and as a skilled pastor, he spiritually calmed the crowd with scriptures from Psalms, and then once the movement ascended, he nodded at Kane.

Kane took both of Veronica's hands in his after she passed her bouquet to Selena. Then he began. "Veronica, all of my life has been filled with joy and happiness, because my parents taught me that my joy was always found in Jesus and my happiness, were moments in life He created just for me. I know, without doubt, He brought you to Louisiana, caused me to find you, and gave me spiritual insight into how you were the rib from my rib. And all to gift me a form of happiness that would last a lifetime. This day and forever, I vow to honor and cherish you. When you're down, feeling depleted by the world, or feel you have no reason to smile, I will remind you of this day. The day, when I promised to make everything all right. Because as sure as the Son is causing the sun to shine, I'll fight to make things right because you, my darling, are forever mine. My love will never waiver, or my support will never linger. My eyes will permanently be fixated on you, and my ears opened and listening whenever you speak. I'll never leave space for you to wonder, doubt, or fear. And I will always cover, protect, provide, and consider you as long as we both shall live.

Kane didn't wait for Selena to wipe Veronica's tears. He took his handkerchief from his jacket and wiped her tears until she smiled.

"Aww," the entire crowd echoed.

"My darling Kane, I have something so rare in you as I have searched all my days to belong, and when you found me, I knew I had finally found my place and my space. You will never have to question my love for you. You will never have to wonder if I'd leave you. And if by chance God calls me home before He calls you, you must always know that the only One who could ever make me leave what I have and have found in you is Jesus. But as long as He continues to lend me breath in this body, I will respect, honor, obey, cherish, and love you with every ounce of my heart's strength and capabilities. My body is yours. My soul is intertwined with yours. And I will always stand in agreement with you. As sure as the Lord promised to be in the midst of two who agree, I promise to always be present in the presence of our Lord, touching and agreeing—you and me. I will always render prayers on your behalf and be the helpmeet you've seen in your mom, and I've seen in mine until death due us apart."

"All that's left for me to do is pray." Pastor Strong asked the crowd to bow and point their hands towards the couples, then began, "Father, You have heard the vows of these your people. Solidify their vows as a staple upon their hearts that they may not ever sin against one another.

Be God in their lives, righteous King, and judge, and cause them to stand as a united front against all the evils in this world. Father, we who witness the love between these two couples, stand in awe of Your greatness. We stand amazed by the power of love, and we promise to cover them in prayer, counsel them when they are in need, cry with them when they cry, laugh with them when they laugh, but most of all, worship with them because You are worthy to be worshipped. We love You, Lord, and we praise Your holy name, in Jesus' name we pray, Amen."

"Amen," everyone said, and the crowd stood with handclaps and shouts.

"By the power vested in me by the good ole state of Louisiana, I now pronounce y'alls married now. You are indeed husbands and wives, and kiss your brides."

As Kane and Vance planted kisses on their brides, the crowd roared with chants of praises. Steven immediately lifted his arms to indicate to the musicians it was time. The music started, and the ensemble began to sing with Lady Antwine leading this time.

♪♫When God designs a love that's great for you
It's most sensational a feeling overdue.
When He joins two hearts as one an expression of His grace
It's so miraculous a forever space.
So today, we witness how great God is,
We see the measure of His grace,
Remnants of His peace,
And the blessing of true love.
This day, we witness how great God is
We see the magnitude of hope.
Proven plan of Adam of Eve
And the blessing of real love.♪♫

The wedding party exited the space as the crowd cheered and clapped, but Austin stayed behind. They had been pre-instructed to go straight to the front lawn for pictures. Jessica jumped right into action, making an announcement. "Guests, would you please journey back to the lounge and mingle, as our hostesses will direct each of you to your dinner tables."

The crowd began moving around greeting each other, and others were in a hurry to be seated or to get their hands on that delicious hors d'oeuvres.

"Come here, Austin," Jessica demanded through the microphone, as she pulled Hope, who had come to greet her, close to her.

"Austin Davenport, you're late. This is Hope Gatlin. I need you two to partner up and be my assistants. First, I need you to make sure that the photographers get all the pictures you know I'd like, Hope. And Austin, I need you to bodyguard Hope and make sure that what she says goes. Do you both understand?"

"Yes, ma'am," they answered.

"What you waiting for? With your lagging behind. Austin grab her hand and escort her to your assignment," Jessica fussed.

"Yes, ma'am," Austin answered and grabbed Hope's hand following the command he'd received.

A bolt of electricity struck him. He wasn't sure if Hope felt what he'd felt, but something happened.

As they walked hand in hand towards the front, Austin's heart said, for the moment, his hand was right where he needed to be. He laced his fingers into hers.

Hope looked up into Austin's eyes and smiled.

"I'm sorry that we weren't properly introduced before we were thrust into a relationship. I mean a working relationship."

"Oh, it's okay. Mrs. Booth is no-nonsense, and when she wants something done, it happens."

"I see."

"Well, if it helps, I'm Hope Gatlin. I work for the law offices of Jackson and Booth, and I'm twenty-three years old."

"Okay, that helps. I'm Austin Davenport. I work for the NFL, and I'm twenty-two. And since we'll be together all night, I must warn you that I love to dance, and I plan on dancing you out of those stilettos."

"But you didn't ask me if I had a date?"

"I didn't need to. Because if Mrs. Booth is as keen as I suppose, she made you my date, and I'm more than excited."

"Alright then, let's get these pictures behind us so I can show you a thing or two."

"Girl, there's not much of anything I haven't already seen, but by all means, I won't stop you from showing me anything you like, my Hope."

"Your Hope?"

"That's what I said because, from the looks of things, this is the ideal setup."

"All I have to say to that is, let the fun begin. But it will have to wait until our job is done."

Austin smiled but looked up right into the face of Selena.

CHAPTER 25

Everyone was seated at their dinner table, and all the guests were patiently awaiting the speeches of the best men and the matrons of honor, which was next on the menu's program section. As with the wedding, Jasmine and Vance's attendants approached the microphone first.

Austin cleared his throat. Most of the small chatter going on at the tables stopped. "Good evening everyone. My name is Austin, and I'm that dude's best man. I knew from the moment he met Jasmine that she was the one. Dude texted me and said, "Man, I think I'm staring at the future, Mrs. Vance Kimbrel. Now, big dude doesn't usually fall that fast, so I knew hands down, Jasmine had to be one of the finest chicks ever created."

The entire crowd started laughing, causing Austin to pause.

"Well, when big dude brought Jasmine home, I knew he'd found his rib. Jasmine, I just want you to know that Vance has never looked at a woman the way he looks at you in all my years of knowing him. And I, for one, always thought love, at first sight, was a joke until today. My prayer, and yes, I said a prayer, Vance, is that you two live out your best lives together and despite, and that you hurry up and make me an uncle. Cheers."

The crowd laughed and clapped.

Then he handed the microphone to Jade.

"Jas, I am so proud of the woman you've become. Like Austin, there are just some things that give us all the affirmation and conformation we needed to tell you've found him. Girl, when you stopped shopping like a crazed maniac, I knew this was him. Anyone who can make Jasmine Booth scale back when it comes to shopping has to be a king."

"Now, that's the truth," Jasper Sr. yelled, causing an already roaring-with-laughter crowd to get louder.

Jade continued, "I know that the Lord makes no mistakes, and what He has joined together will never be put asunder. It is my prayer that He continues to bless you both and that His joy will forever be your strength. Cheers"

"Hear, hear!" The crowd shouted, then the microphone was passed to J.J.

"My dearest brother, big brother, I might add. You have been much more than I would have hoped for in a brother and a business partner. And there's nothing I would have ever wanted more than to see the smile on your face now. I thought the best thing that could've ever happened to you was being my brother, but I realize it's becoming Veronica's husband."

Just as J.J. wiped a tear from his eye, Kane was doing the same.

"I know that God has so much more in store for you two, and I'm happy to be a part of your journey. Big bro, I'll always be here for you both, and I promise that Jade and I will always have your backs. Cheers."

"Hear, hear," the crowd yelled and dried their eyes as well.

"I guess they saved the best for last." Selena giggled, and their family clapped.

"No one could have told me last year that I'd be standing here giving a toast to my cousin. Veronica, I know that God works in mysterious ways, and I also know that there is power in love. What He has done through you both lets me know that all those of us who are single needs are hope and a willing heart."

"Yes," Aunt Valerie yelled at Selena.

"Will all the single people in this room stand up?" Selena asked, and singles started rising all over the room.

"We the single people vow to look out for you, never harm what you have, and babysit when you need us." Everyone laughed.

"But most of all, we vow to wait until God sends us the one He has created just for us, and when we find her or are found by him, we promise to hold on tight just like you have to Kane and be determined through anything and everything to fight for our love. May God bless you, may He keep you, and may He always cause the sun and His Son to shine upon you."

"Hear, hear," the crowd cheered.

Jessica stood, and Selena handed her the microphone.

"If you all don't mind, my husband would like to say something to his children."

"We don't mind," someone yelled from the crowd.

Jessica hand Jasper Sr. the microphone.

"I am the proudest man on earth. All three of my children have found the love of the lives, and now I'm no longer responsible for them." Jasper laughed, and their guests did too.

"On a serious note, you three men are strong men of valor, and we," he pointed in the direction of their parents, grandparents, uncles, and friends, "are so proud of you all. No man in this room will tell you that marriage is easy. We will not lie to you, but we will tell you that if you make the Lord the CEO and the COO of your marriage, He'll help you always make the right decisions. And I know sometimes the wrong decisions will seem easiest to make, but I promise if you just go with God...and do things His way, you will never fail yourself or each other. I love you all, and if you have learned nothing else from your and me mother, I pray you've got a firm understanding that two is always better than one. When you agree, you have the power to move mountains. I love you, Booth-Kimbrel's clan."

"We love you," all three of the couples yelled at Jasper, and they all came to hug their dad and father-in-love, and Jessica joined her family.

The entire crowd clapped and joined in with their joy. There was nothing like a black family who put God first and understood the power of love towards each other and those God had created for them to cover.

CHAPTER 26

Damon wiped his hands down his pants. They were sweating like he was getting ready to play the championship game, and he was the star player. It had taken him a couple of hours to get to Mrs. Booth to tell her his plan, but when he finally got to her, it was all worth the wait.

She assured him they were the family of surprises, and if anyone could help him pull off his surprise, it was the Booth/Kimbrel gang. She'd already given DJ Love all of the definite instructions as well as Jade, and—of course—Jade was ready.

Anytime love was involved, she was just as much ready as Jessica was.

The entire family was more than willing to put aside some of their time for Selena's surprise. They all had grown to love her as if she were one of the sisters.

Jessica nodded, and the show got on the road.

"ALL RIGHT. Enough of the crying. Now y'all come on clap your hands for this awesome family. I'd like the brides and their grooms to hit the floor for their first dance," D J Love said, and the couples obeyed.

The orchestra began playing "Be the One," by Sinead Harnett, and Jade moved to the microphone and began singing as the couples started dancing. It was definitely a moment made for movies. Yet again, there was no dry eye in the place after the two couples danced as if this moment was choreographed.

Kane and Vance swirled Veronica and Jasmine around the room like princesses who had found their princes. The crowd was in awe of the love and closeness of the couples. When the song came to an end, the guests stood and applauded the two most beautiful couples, most of them had seen since Jayla's and Jamecia's wedding.

The crowd applauded them.

Both Jayla and Jamecia came to hug Jasmine and Veronica. After they laughed and giggled for a moment, Jasmine and Jayla declared that if you got married with them, you had the wedding of a lifetime. And although Jamecia and Veronica thought they were two of the most insane and arrogant chicks, they'd decided to allow them to have their moment.

For sure, out of all of them, both Jayla and Jasmine were the babies and were as spoiled as spoil could be. But the good thing about them, they were great shoppers who bought great gifts.

After a couple of small clustered gatherings, DJ Love began playing, "If You Let Me," by the same artist as others joined the dance floor.

Damon saw a wink from Jessica, and he quickly found Selena, standing talking with Rufus's mom, Catilina, and her mom, Vashti. He excused her and then pulled Selena on the dance floor and into his arms.

I've wanted you right here all night.

He looked into her eyes.

Their bodies swayed like two people who had been dancing together for a lifetime. Selena closed her eyes as her mind drifted to the same dance floor in the middle of the Bahamas, where they'd been dancing as if they were two in love. The way he held her, the way she felt his move in his mind before it registered with his feet was more than a coincidence.

Interrupting her silent thoughts, Damon pulled her close, causing Selena to look straight into his eyes.

"Selena, will you let me?" he mouthed as they grooved together. Feeling the music, the passion, and the heat just like that night on their vacation double date. Both of them worried that their significant other would discern the tension they felt from one another. But this time, neither of them had to worry about anyone noticing the chemistry between them. They didn't have to worry if it looked like they wanted each other. And, they didn't have anyone to answer to but themselves.

Damon interrupted her thoughts again. "You didn't answer me. Will you let me?"

"Damon, is that what you really want? You have the perfect chance to walk away from me, from this, and never look back again."

"Selena, this is also the perfect chance, right now, to prove to you that if you let me love you, I'll love you like no one has ever loved you before. Baby, if you just put your focus and attention all on me, I'll be to you exactly what you need in a man and show you that when God connects you with the missing part of yourself, you cherish, love, adore, and treat it better than you've treated yourself. So you won't ever lose it, mistreat it, or abuse it. You'll simply show that piece all the love that you've been waiting to give the one you were chosen to give love to."

He twirled her around and pulled her back into a tight embrace.

Selena gasped.

Pure sexual tension. Lord, this must be what Veronica felt when she ran like Forrest Gump.

Damon spun her out again and this time he brought her gently into him. This time, Damon could feel the pounding of Selena's heart. He pressed a soft kiss on her neck and remembering that he was in a room filled with Christians, he definitely didn't need his flesh trying to disrespect the space.

He blew a breath to calm his body and his mind.

"Selena, the way your heart is beating right now is how I want it to beat forever. Just at the sound of my name, I want your heart to do exactly what it's doing right now." And at that moment, Damon couldn't help himself. He captured Selena's lips and kissed her with the fervent passion he'd held in his heart since the day he saw her walking through his high school's halls. Since the day he'd walked into her home with Rufus and saw her standing at the kitchen sink in a Cowboys' jersey. Or the day she came back to Dade County and stepped out her car to walk into her abuela's house. So many times, he'd dreamt of holding and kissing her like she belonged to him. And now, to have this moment planned out just for him, he wasn't going to dare miss the opportunity to plant his lips on her beautiful full lips and capture them like an angler catching the biggest fish in the ocean.

He allowed her to catch her breath and went right back in almost forgetting what he was about to do until he heard the next song begin to play.

Because it was scripted and carefully planned out, the orchestra began playing, and Jade took to the microphone again and started singing H.E.R., "My Song."

Jessica's thoughtful plan to clear the dance floor had gone so smooth Selena never noticed when the dance floor was cleared. Neither did Damon. He just knew what song he wanted to propose to the love of his life and he'd asked Jade beforehand.

The only people on the dance floor were Damon and Selena, and it was enchanting and magical. He swayed with her in his arms as Jade drew out so much passion in the song. When Selena finally noticed she and Damon were alone, tears began to run down her face.

Damon kissed her tears and kept dancing with the love of his life, and as Jade ad-libbed, he twirled her around. When he stopped, he was on his knee with a beautiful diamond in his hand.

"Selena, will you be my forever song? Will you let me love you like you've never been loved before? Will you let me cover you just as Christ covers His church? Will you let me give my life in place of you giving yours? Die for you? And forever cry with you?"

"Yes, yes, yes, yes, to all of that. Yes!" she cried, and he stood, lifted Selena in his arms, and swung her around.

Now the crowd was again roaring with cheers.

When he replaced her feet on the floor, both brides along with Veronica, Valerie, her mother Vashti, here mother-in-love Catilina, and her Abuela Marita, rushed in to hug her. Damon quickly moved to the side and was greeted by the grooms, her father, Dr. Aaron Cox, and her uncles by marriage and love—James and Jasper Booth Sr.

CHAPTER 27

Of course, Jessica, Valerie, and Vashti were immediately ready to plan the next wedding, but thankfully Damon felt her heart and pulled his future bride back onto the dance floor. All the love songs had now been replaced with Louisiana line dance music and zydeco.

Kane pulled Veronica onto the dance floor after she'd changed into a little red dress Jamecia designed as an after-five party-wear for a bride. The dress fit in all the right places and Kane held onto her as if he could lose her.

"Baby, you have made me the happiest woman on earth," she whispered to Kane.

"Girl, you haven't seen anything yet."

"And might I ask what you mean by that, sir?"

"You'll see. I have so much to apologize to you for. I made the wrong decision, and it nearly cost me the love of my life. Baby, I promise I'm going to make sure the baggage I've been carrying will never affect what we have. To be honest, with the my moms help, I'm learning how to appreciate everything God has done for me."

"Baby, I want to help you carry your baggage until we destroy every piece that will cause us to be at odds. I was able to help my cousin, but I promise you I was so miserable without you, Kane. You never realize how much you desire and need a person in your life until you get in a space where their presence is missing. I totally got in the shower just to cry because I missed you so much."

"I did the same thing. Maybe not like you did, but after J.J. laughed in my face and Moms chewed me out, I closed my office door, turned on my music, and cried. For the first time in my life, it seemed like the wrong decision had cost me everything. I know before I ever make a decision that might cause me to lose you, I'll make it with you. Hands down. I'm not gonna ever be your ex."

They both started laughing when the DJ played "*EX*" by Kiana Ledé.

Veronica kissed Kane. "Well, same here, so don't ever treat me like it and don't ever think I'd do anything to make you want me to be an ex. You are stuck with me forever, homeboy. And even if you tried to leave me, I'd hunt you down, stalk you, and make you see—in some way—that you've made the wrong decision."

"Please don't ever get crazy on me. You just promise you won't be like old girl chasing your brother, and I promise to never make the wrong decision."

"You've got a deal."

"Let's kiss on it, then."

Veronica leaned in and kissed Kane with her whole heart and soul.

EPILOGUE

I t had been two months since their whirlwind honeymoon, and Kane wanted to do something to show all of their friends how much they were appreciated: since they'd all played a part in the wonderful double wedding.

Everyone had agreed upon doing a couples weekend at J.J. and Jade's house. They had enough bedrooms to sleep an entire basketball team in their house, but J.J. and Kane had gotten this wild hair to build a huge barn. It housed a wide open den including a dance floor, a bar, and an open kitchen with twenty rooms upstairs, twenty downstairs, and each room had a bathroom.

Enough room to play UNO and spades and have a big ole weekend blast. Regina had been hired to create each couple a huge welcome basket for their rooms that included: snacks, wine, wineglasses, fruit, and a special gift handpicked by Veronica and Kane.

And of course, Jasmine and Vance couldn't be outdone, so they purchased everyone a set of different colored pajamas with their initials embroidered on the right side and a pair of matching slippers.

Jade and J.J. bought everyone t-shirts so that the women whose shirts were pink, could play a game of kickball against the blue-shirted men. They'd planned everything out, crossing every t and dotting every

i. Even Pastor Strong and First Lady Destiny had made this event one of their vacation Sundays, and Destiny vowed to use this as her birthday weekend.

They all were excited and up for the pastor and his wife hanging out because they were so cool.

Veronica pulled out the paper with each couple on the list.

Even she had to laugh at herself for separating the not-marrieds and making sure she knew to put them in separate rooms. Now Jasmine and Vance shacked before they got married, but if she could help it, everyone on this trip would respect the fact that Pastor Strong and Lady Destiny were here as well.

If it hadn't been for them, she had to admit to Kane and herself that she would have closed her eyes and acted like a blind lady who saw no evil and heard none either. As the guests began to pour in, she checked each of them off the list, gave them their room assignment and keys, but made sure to tell them to meet in the den at five-thirty on the nose.

By four-forty-five, all of their guests were in their rooms as some of the early old heads had already made their way to the den. At five-thirty, everyone could be accounted for. Kane stood with Veronica by his side.

"Veronica and I would like to thank each and every one of you for showing up and being our friends. We consider each of you family and you each have played such an important role in our lives. We wanted to make sure that we had all of you in one space when we announced," he looked at Veronica and she nodded, "We will be welcoming a baby girl or boy in the next eight months."

"Yeah!" Cheers went up all over the room.

"It's about time someone made me a grandpa," Jasper yelled.

"Hallelujah!" Jessica screamed.

"Aww," cooed Veronica, "we knew y'all would be happy. Now, we are going to turn things over to our other hosts."

"Hello," Jade and J.J. said together.

"Before we get started, I would like to give J.J. something he's been looking for." Jade handed J.J. a Nike shoebox. He was certain that she'd found the pair of brand new Nike Air VaporMax Flyknit 3's he'd been looking for all over town and the internet. Everyone watched intensely as he removed the tape that held the box down to open it up.

J.J. moved the paper and stared at Jade.

Instead of his dream shoes, inside there were one pair of pink and one pair of aqua Nike Air Max 270 Extreme for toddlers.

He looked at the shoes and then back at Jade. His hands were shaking so bad until Kane grabbed the box to see what his brother saw.

"Jade, are we—no y'all—having twins? Are you pregnant?" Kane screamed.

"Surprise," Jade yelled and jumped up and down. "I got you J.J. I got you. You're so speechless, you still can't talk."

And J.J. just started crying.

Now Jade was crying and so was everyone else in the room. She had paid J.J. back for giving her the surprise wedding, and the joke was not only on him, but his parents as well. Jessica and Jasper Sr. cried like someone had just lost their life.

Pastor Strong stood. "This, my brothers and sisters is what the joy of the Lord looks like. Even though you may be crying, you are so full of joy on the inside until you can't even explain yourself or the joy you feel. Come on, y'all stop crying and praise the Lord for this wonderful extension to our FTC family."

"Everyone was wiping tears and yelling, 'Thank You, Jesus.'"

J.J. picked Jade up off the floor in his arms and kissed her until both he and she exploded with tears again. The Booth family had three babies on the way and no one could have been happier than Jasper Sr. and Jessica.

Selena hugged her cousin first, and everyone took turns hugging both Veronica and Jade. As soon as the excitement had worn off, and everyone was back down from the high, Pastor Strong looked at Selena, Damon, Carlotta, Lyden, Isha, Chance, Melissa, and Sean and said, "This is the perfect chance to meet God at the altar and make us as happy as these two have. Who's next?"

And the entire room began screaming in laughter.

The End

THE GUEST LIST

Rooms -up 1& 2: Jade and J.J.; Veronica and Kane
  Rooms -up 3 & 4: Jasmine and Vance; Jayla and Dwight
  Rooms-up 5 & 6: Selena and Damon; Hope and Austin (G2)(M2)
  Rooms-up 7 & 8: Carlotta and Lyden; Isha and Chance(G2)(M2)
  *(The mental note to let these two girls have a room together and their guys together because they hadn't gotten married yet.)
  Rooms-up 9 & 10: Jamecia and Jacob; Priscilla and Steven
  Rooms-up 11: Regina and Nathan;
  Rooms-d 1 & 2: Destiny and Pastor Roderick; Sheila and Jake
  Rooms-d 3 & 4: Stephanie and Carlos; Jessica and Jasper Sr.
  Rooms-d 5 & 6: Vashti and Aaron; Felicia and Dean
  Rooms-d 7 & 8: Carol and Ivan; Tammy and Reginald
  Rooms-d 9 & 10: Tawonna and Daryl; Dallas and Tajdrick
  Rooms-d 11: Jennifer and Baxter
  Rooms-d 12 & 13 Melissa and Sean (Newest deacon in the church who she's dating. (Separate rooms!)

DEAR READER

If you enjoyed *The Wrong Decision*, Book 2 of A Louisiana Love Series, try reading The Right Choice Book 1. Or go to where it all started... A Louisiana Christmas Books 1& 2: Love Me Again and Never Looking Back. You can read them apart, but I promise you'll get the best of these families by reading those two books as well.

Please consider writing a book *review* on any platform where reviews are available. Book reviews are so pivotal in helping authors gain readership and so much more, and I would genuinely appreciate it.

It does not have to be long. You can write a few sentences to express or describe how you felt about this book and that would be awesome.

One more thing...

Would you please help me by recommending this book to your family members and friends? Also, recommend it to book clubs, your church members, ask your local library to get a copy, share it on your social media pages, and with your church libraries.

PLEASE JOIN MY MAILING LIST
BY VISITING:

Danyelle's Mailing List

Notes (Songs mentioned or written in The Wrong Decision):
"Ave Maria," originated from Ellen's Third Song, written by Franz Schubert in 1825. The song is the Latin name of the prayer Hail Mary with words by Sir Walter Scott and music composed by Franz Liszt in some versions and by Franz Schubert in others.

"Glory To His Name," written by Elisha A. Hoffman and musically arranged by John H. Stockton.

"Open Heaven" as sung by gospel sensation, Maranda Curtis.

"Be the One," and "If You Let Me" by Sinead Harnett.

"Forever and Ever," by Danyelle Scroggins

"God's Picture of Joy," by Danyelle Scroggins

"The Blessing of Real Love," by Danyelle Scroggins

"EX" by Kiana Ledé.

THE RIGHT CHOICE
PROLOGUE

January 26th, Grand Cane, Louisiana. Jasmine sat on the balcony of her recently married brother's home and cried. She had no desire to be bothered or deal with anyone. All she wanted was to be left alone. It had been exactly three weeks since she left California pledging to never return to the city, nor to Vance.

She'd seen all she needed to see. And no one, not even her father—who had tried twice since her return—could convince her of anything different. Vance was no good, and not worth her time.

The only bad thing...their families were tied together forever, and there was nothing she could do about it. Uncle James was married to Vance's mother. Her older brother, Kane, was eager to plan the wedding of a lifetime to Vance's sister, Veronica, especially, after all the drama they had endured.

It would be too selfish to allow what transpired between her and Vance to alter her feelings towards Valerie and Veronica. And it would be childish to walk around like they'd done something to her, when they had done nothing at all. So the best resolution was to stay hidden at J.J. and Jade's house, and pretend like no one existed except her and them.

Jasmine was beginning to think her father was right after all. No woman should move in with a man who hadn't married them, or play wife to a man who wasn't her husband.

For months, she'd believed that Vance loved her.

She cleaned, cooked, washed, and did everything a woman should do for a man except sex. At least she was smart enough to hold on to something until after they were married. But that still didn't help her hurting heart.

Now it was time to think about Jasmine.

Not Vance.

Not her father's business.

But Jasmine.

As soon as she could muster enough strength to talk about what happened and to answer the questions from her family, she would come out of hiding and face the music. Until then, she would cry behind the pain that came from the wrong voice and choice.

At least, until she was all cried out.

৩৫৩

December 29, California. Jasmine sat on a huge fluffy pillow in the corner of Vance's two-bedroom apartment. It had been quite the task convincing her family that their living together in California was best for them. But for some, it still hadn't worked. No one saw the move coming, and the surprise of it all provoked some heated conversations.

For Jasmine, some days the conversations still hurt. And today was one of those days. Sure, they had a valid argument. She'd fallen in love really quick with Vance. But what wasn't to love about him? He was charming, smart, loyal, and he was a Christian. Not in words only, he truly had a heart for God. And if she was right, he loved her.

Jasmine rose from the plush sofa and walked to the huge window overlooking the pool. With her shoulder pressed against the wall, she gazed at what appeared to be a happy family enjoying their day. Sort of how her family was the day after Christmas for Kane's birthday. All smiles until she and Vance made their big announcement.

Jasmine sighed. *I'm here now.* California was nothing like she thought it would be, but hanging out with Vance in his collegiate atmosphere was fun. Even his friends embraced her. The only thing she couldn't get used to—the groupies. The girls who hung around athletes praying to land a husband before they went into the league. Here, they ran in cliques, dressed in skimpy clothes, and were relentless when they found their target. They couldn't care less if the target had a woman at his side. To them— she was replaceable.

Thank God for Vance's no-disrespect clause. Only God knew whether it was for their good or hers. The first time Jasmine saw how disrespectful they were, she vowed to lay claws if they ever tried her. Instead, Vance blocked her own mode of act-right, like he was a line-backer protecting her, the quarterback. He demanded their respect, but then again was she still worth respecting? She'd gone against the grain of everything her parents taught.

Jasmine sighed and shifted her weight to her other leg. Word for word, over and over, she rehearsed their last conversation like the lyrics to a bad song.

"You mean to tell me that my boys have more respect for marrying the woman first before they live together. And my girl is running off to live with a fiancé like that's perfectly fine?" Jasper Sr. yelled like he was losing it.

"Dad, I'm not Jasper or Kane and I'm grown!" she yelled back.

"You might be grown, but you're making a childish decision. I'd prefer he marry you first and then y'all go wherever y'all want to go. Heck, you can go live in the woods of Cambodia if you want. But at least you'd be married and God can bless you."

"Dad, we are grown, and Vance and I have enough self-control to live together and not do the things married people do. And even if we did, Dad, we are two grown consenting adults who have a right to make their own decisions."

"If you were, we wouldn't be having this conversation. I believe I'm talking to a child who is out of her mind. You're going to leave your job, home, and everything you've built to go live in an overpriced two-bedroom get-up until y'all decide to get married. Absolutely ridiculous!"

"Jasper, enough! You two have been going back and forwards for the last

five minutes, and I've listened to you both and I'm sick of it. We have done our part, Jasper. We have raised these children in the way they should go, and at some point, we have to give them room to make their own choices." Jessica pulled a crying Jasmine into her arms.

"Jessica, she's making a dumb mistake, baby," Jasper ranted.

"Dad, it's my dumb mistake to make, and maybe I'm more like you than J.J. and Kane," Jasmine countered.

"I've never hit you, Jasmine Booth, but you'd better be quiet right now before I—"

"Before you what, Jasper?" Jessica asked. "You'd better shut this down and now before you both make me mad. And you both know, you don't want that. Now, Jasmine is old enough to make her own decisions, and although we may not like them, they are hers to make. And Jasmine, no matter how crazy your dad is being, you will never disrespect your father in any way. Do you understand me?"

"Yes ma'am," Jasmine whined.

"If you and Vance have decided to make this type of move, you do know you are making it without our blessing but with us praying. We have witnessed many men use the cow up and then decide they don't want her. That's all we are saying. But this is the life and body God gave you. If you make the choice to abuse it, that's you. You alone will have to live and deal with the choices you make. But you will still be our daughter, and we will love you no less. Now go wash your face and go home to pack."

"I do love you both." The last thing Jasmine said to her parents' before leaving. Almost hating she'd ever came. She knew they were disappointed, and now she was the cause of them being angry with one another. Her mother's eyes were the proof that Dad was in for a tongue-lashing like never before. And usually, it was her stance to protect her daddy from her fire breathing, no-nonsense, mother. But not that day.

Jasmine blew out another deep breath.

She hated to even think of her parents arguing, especially when the subject of their disagreement was her. She'd prefer it be one of her brothers or even Jade. No matter what, she wasn't changing her mind. What if she stayed and lost the best thing that could have ever happened to her? *Vance needs me, and I need him.*

Jasmine began to cry. "Lord, they don't know I've been suffering in silence," she mumbled through sniffles. "I went to work everyday, almost killing myself trying to prove I earned my job based upon work ethic and not my family ties."

She pulled a tissue from the coffee table, blew her nose, and closed her eyes laying her head in her hands.

Jasmine hated the stigma of being the Booth princess. She hated feeling like others thought her job was given instead of earned. She wanted others to see her as a mastered leveled businesswoman who made good decisions and wise choices concerning job, life, and her future. *A boss lady.*

But somehow the stench of being the Booths' princess and Vance's lady, was now overshadowing everything.

Jasmine turned away from the window and jumped.

"Vance, you startled me. When did you come in?"

"A few seconds ago. I kind of felt like I would scare you but I didn't want to interrupt your thoughts. Are you okay, Jasmine?"

"Yes, just thinking."

"About the last conversation you had with your parents again?"

"Yeah, sort of. Well, yeah."

"Do you want to go back to Louisiana?"

"And leave you?"

"Yes, that would definitely mean you'd be leaving me. But I know you've been troubled by how things went. I don't want to be the bad blood between you and your parents and truth is, I understand them perfectly."

"Vance, I know but it's not you. I needed to grow up and this was a grown-up move." Jasmine made air quotations. "No one except Mom, Jade, and Veronica know we sleep in separate rooms, and that we are keeping things holy. But, I'm not concerned. I'm staying right here until you go to training camp like we planned."

"Well, we could go ahead and get married."

"Vance, we are fine just like we are. It hurts that I've let them down, but as long as God knows, He's all that matters."

"Okay, boss-lady, I'm riding with you, but at the same time, I'm praying for us."

"That's all I can ask of you. I love you, Vance."

"I love you, Jasmine Booth. The future Mrs. V. Kimbrel."

"Sounds good to me."

COMING SOON: THE PERFECT CHANCE

Selena was so happy watching all the comradely in the room after the announcement of Veronica and Jade's pregnancies. The Booth family was expanding, and like the reverend said, it was right before their eyes. She wondered if her mom and dad would have even a portion of Jasper and Jessica's happy. Because neither she nor her brother Bandarees whom she affectionately called Bubbee, had children.

As a matter of fact, she couldn't seem to keep a husband long enough to get pregnant. Then again, she was thankful that she didn't get pregnant for her deceased husband, Rufus. She was now a rich widow, and the only good thing that had articulated from her marriage was a new relationship with Damon.

She'd always called him, Crawl, his street nickname, but had found out since Rufus' death that he was an undercover police detective who had been in love with her since high school. Long story short, Damon proposed at the wedding of her cousin, and their first event as a couple was a thank you retreat at the retreat center that her cousin's husband and brother built.

After she hugged both women, she made her way back to the sofa beside the man she was beginning to love. Of course, she'd be foolish to believe that she'd said yes to a man she loved. He actually meant a great deal to her, but love was truly not in her forecast.

Unbeknown to her, many women married men who they weren't head over heels in love with.

She tried the love overboard thing with Rufus, to only get beat and become a wealthy widow of a man who cared more about himself than those who loved him. This time, she was doing things the other way around.

This man, holding on to her proudly, loved her like she loved Rufus. All she had to do was tell herself to appreciate what she's never had until she really started appreciating him and the love he gave.

For Selena, it was the perfect chance that she'd been praying for all of her life. Even now, she was still praying for the ideal opportunity to prove to God that she wasn't the selfish, self-loathing human she'd been in the past who self-sabotaged everything He'd ever tried to do for her.

Although many may not understand, she knew that Damon was a gift from God, and she would—as long as she lived—remembered that the blessing that comes from the Lord are those that make you rich and add no sorrow. And that sorrow always found her in every single relationship she's ever had when she opened her heart and her legs, at the same time.

Like most of the other times, the sexual tension was there, and so was the attraction. But this time, she was leading with the Spirit of God and not the spirit of lust.

Damon looked at her and smiled.

That's the one thing I'm so glad God didn't do, let people read thoughts.

Selena smiled back and patted him on his hand, turning her attention back to Pastor Strong, who'd just asked all the singles who would be next to get married. One mind told her to roll her eyes so everyone could stop looking at her, but when she looked up, Austin Davenport was looking directly at her as if he was trying to read her expression.

Austin was a good dude, but he was way too young for her to get involved with. She'd spent some time with him in the hospital after his and Vance's traumatic event, but she'd come to the decision that they could be nothing but friends. By the way, Austin was glaring at her now, he hadn't gotten the memo.

She laughed like the others to get Austin off her trail; and smooth the mind of Damon so he wouldn't rush her. The rush-job engagement was more than enough. Heck, she'd just put her husband in the ground, so if he'd be okay with her riding the widow wave for a little while, she'd make her mind up eventually.

"Awe pastor, don't rush them. Whenever the heat gets hot enough, they'll be running to that altar. Trust me," Kane said, patting pastor Strong on the shoulder.

Thank God for small favors, Kane.

Selena winked at him because she and he had discussed fully what she was feeling and not feeling. Kane was a good ear, and although he didn't give her any advice except, trust God, that was enough to give her permission to let God be God and her His servant. Only moving when the Master said so.

Now her cousin was back before them.

"We've brought you all to this place to share how blessed we are because of you but to also give you a chance as couples to embrace partnership, unity, and friendship. I believe that these are the three entities that will carry you to a fullness of joy in marriage."

"Yes," Jasper Sr. yelled out.

"Thanks, father-in-love, at least you have my back," Veronica bumped fist with him causing everyone to laugh. "I think that we've gone above and beyond to make this a special weekend. I started on Thursday night to give you all a full two days to enjoy all the activities. So tonight, Jade is going before you with a schedule. Don't worry about writing down what she'll tell you because she's already put it on your nightstand. Let's welcome, Jade."

They all began to clap and cheer Jade to the front.

Jade threw her hand to hush them, "I'm so glad that Veronica came up with this and with the help of Jasmine, we've created a schedule that will bless you and maximize your time here."

The room lit up in applause again.

"This is what we decided to do...tonight, we are going to give you a chance as couples to tour the lawns, enjoy the views, mingle, and relax with your significant other until dinner time at seven-thirty. Then we will all meet at the tables where the waiters will serve us and ensure that we are good and full. After dinner, we will join in gender sessions for one hour, from nine to ten. Our session leaders will be the lovely First Lady Destiny Strong and the awesome Dwight Esplanade."

Claps and cheers erupted again.

"And after the sessions, we will give you a moment to do whatever you and your mate want to do...and if you are apart of the crews who have to separate, please remember to respect your roommate and that we all must be up at seven-thirty for breakfast. Is this okay with each of you?"

"It's perfect," they responded.

"Okay, you're dismissed until dinner," Jade threw up her arms and waved at them.

"Old folks, we are going to play a couple of hands of spades, any of you care to join?" James asked the younger couples.

"No, Sir, y'all do y'all," J.J. answered his uncle, and most of the younger couples headed for the back yard.

There were three pools, four fire pit sitting sections, a lake with ten jet skis, an adult miniature golf space, and a walking trail that spanned over ten miles around the noted areas.

Selena and Damon decided to sit by the pool and put their feet in.

"Baby, I'm so glad you invited me. I believe this will be an unforgettable weekend."

"I'm glad you came to be my guest. Anytime these people put anything together, it's definitely done in the spirit of excellence. And, I didn't want to be here by myself."

"I'm glad you didn't. I was becoming a little afraid after I hadn't heard from you last week. I really wanted to give you all the time you needed to process what's going on between us. And another thing, I didn't want to rush you into marriage, but I did want to state a claim onto the woman I've been waiting on since forever."

"Thank you for giving me time. I just want to let Rufus get far behind me before I just jumped up and got married or even in a relationship. Trust me, I know when I've been presented with the perfect chance. I won't make you wait too long, Damon, and I'll be honest with you."

"That's all I can ask you for, Selena."

OTHER BOOKS BY DANYELLE SCROGGINS

Destiny's Decision

More Than Diamonds

The E Love Series

Enduring Love

Enchanting Love

Everlasting Love

Extraordinary Love

Extravagant Love

The Power Series Rebirth

Graced After The Pain

Grace Restored

Grace Realized

Grace Revealed

Made in the USA
Columbia, SC
26 September 2024

42437766R00114